When Aloha Means Goodbye

When Aloha Means Goodbye

a noa webster mystery

Elyn Aviva

WHEN ALOHA MEANS GOODBYE: A Noa Webster Mystery

Copyright © 2006 by Pilgrims Process, Inc.

ISBN: 978-0-9749597-9-5

Library of Congress Control Number: 2006904354

Printed in the United States of America

0 9 8 7 6 5 4 3 2

Set in Minion Pro 11 pt over 14 pt

Dedication:

To Estebán Romero, Noa's greatest fan

Other books by Elyn Aviva:

Following the Milky Way: A Pilgrimage on the Camino de Santiago

The Journey: A Novel of Pilgrimage and Spiritual Quest

Dead End on the Camino: A Noa Webster Mystery

One

Pot-bellied men panting behind long-legged nymphs in string bi-
kinis, streets lined with overpriced shops catering to free-spending
tourists, droves of rental cars clogging the narrow roads—this was
Maui. Maui at Christmas. And Maui at Christmas, I was beginning to
realize, was not my idea of paradise.

The only bright spot had been Alex. When I first met him in the
hotel bar I had had my doubts, but he turned out to be a delightful
companion. Now, however, even that bright spot was tarnished. Or
should I say, stained.

But I suppose I should start at the beginning of the story—the
beginning, at any rate, of my involvement in it. As I learned later, the
story really began almost two centuries earlier.

I had gotten up early and gone for a leisurely stroll on the deserted beach, enjoying the luscious mango-colored sunrise over *Lanai*, a
small island to the west of Maui. I know the sun rises in the east, but

in Paradise—or at least, in the Pacific—one is often treated to a double sunrise, one in the east and its reflection in the west.

Half-an-hour later, I climbed back over the low ridge of sand to the hotel and selected an ocean-front lounge chair with a prime view of the tiny crescent-shaped island of Molokini and, hopefully, of any humpback whales lurking below the surface and ready to spout. Lulled by the incessant pounding of the surf, I dozed off.

The next thing I knew, someone was softly calling my name. With a start, I opened my eyes. Gazing at me with a slow, seductive smile was Alex. Tan, blue-eyed Alex, muscles rippling subtly across his bronzed chest, sea water glistening in his golden hair. Water puddled around his bare, sandy feet.

"Been swimming?" I asked, then mentally kicked myself for being so trite.

"Snorkeling," he said, in his deep, resonant voice. "The reefs are just off-shore, and the snorkeling here is the best of all the Hawaiian islands. Or so I'm told."

"I've never gone snorkeling," I said. "What's it like?"

"Like nothing else. You're suspended in the middle of a silent, green-blue world, surrounded by dozens of brightly colored parrot fish, yellow tang, angel fish, eels—"

"Do they bite?"

"Not usually," he laughed. "Tell you what, Noa, I'll give you a lesson tomorrow—"

"Sunday?"

"Sure. Why not."

"Sounds good to me," I replied enthusiastically.

"Great. I'll get some peas and bread from the hotel restaurant—the fish love to be fed. They'll even nibble the food out of your hands—but watch out for the sharks!" Seeing my nervous look, he laughed. "Just kidding, Noa. Trust me—no sharks."

He dropped a heavy vinyl beach bag on the lounge chair next to me. A red-tipped snorkel stuck out from the top. "How about some coffee?"

"Kona?"

"For you, nothing but the best!"

He strode off to the open-air bar next to the hotel pool. Yes, pool. Although the Maui Surf Hotel is just a hundred yards from a gorgeous white-sand beach that slopes gently into the crystal-clear water, many of the guests refuse to swim in the ocean. So the hotel provides a large heated pool with none of the discomforts—or vagaries—of nature. A few guests in bathing suits were leaning against the bar, staring out at the ocean; a few others were claiming lounge chairs around the pool.

Soon Alex returned with two steaming mugs of fragrant Kona coffee, grown on the mountain slopes of the nearby Big Island—Hawaii. He moved the beach bag, leaned back on the lounge chair, wiggled his sand-encrusted toes, and sighed.

"This is the life."

"Mmm . . . ." I murmured in agreement, enjoying the gentle ocean breeze caressing my skin, listening to the surf slurping against the shore.

We drank our coffee in appreciative silence. After a minute or two, Alex reached into his beach bag and pulled out a small dark figure. He rubbed his fingers over it absent-mindedly.

"What's that?" I asked.

"Take a look," he said, tossing it to me.

I examined it curiously, intrigued by the ferocious jagged-tooth grimace, the faceted green eyes, the earrings that looked like steel ball bearings. The oversized head was topped with a Mohawk-style headdress ornamented with zigzag ridges. The carving was crude—the arms hung rigidly down, still joined to the thick torso, the legs tapered to a mere suggestion of feet. The dark, unfinished figure seemed to soak up the light around it. Staring at it, I felt a vague uneasiness, as if the glittering eyes were staring back at me malevolently.

With a shiver, I handed it back to Alex. "What is it?"

"Just a tourist souvenir," he replied with a grin.

"A tourist souvenir? Are you sure that's all it is?"

Alex laughed. "Leave it to an anthropologist to give spiritual power to a piece of wood! It's just a *tiki* figure—like you'd find at O'Rourke's Tourist Trap."

"If you say so, but it gives me the willies."

"Well, I'll admit I didn't get it at O'Rourke's, but trust me, it's just a souvenir."

A loud noise startled us, and we both turned around to look. A guest, his back turned towards us, had bumped into a chair, knocking it over.

Suddenly Alex pointed towards the ocean. "Look, Noa! There's a whale!"

I jumped up and shaded my eyes, staring at the sea. "Where?"

"Over there—near Molokini! Can't you see the spout?"

I looked intently for the spume of water but saw nothing. "No. Where?"

"Too late. You missed it. Look—I gotta go. See you later!"

Alex sprinted up the path towards the hotel. What, I wondered, had brought on his abrupt departure? A sudden attack of stomach distress? Puzzled but not unduly concerned, I continued to savor my coffee, staring at the ocean, hoping to catch my first sight of one of the many humpback whales that come to Maui in winter to give birth to their young and frolic in the warm waters. I'd read about the enormous creatures and even heard tapes of their strange, spooky songs; songs that change each year. I very much wanted to see one before I left the island. Maybe I should sign up for a Whale Foundation sightseeing expedition, I mused. In the meantime, I scanned the horizon without success.

About half an hour later Alex had still not returned. Sweet-talking playboy, charming, superficial Adonis. He really wasn't my type, I mused, unlike my on-again, off-again boyfriend Peter, who was the kind of man—intellectual, ambivalent, ascetic—that I usually found attractive. But Alex was so good looking I could easily ignore his lack of depth. Wryly, I realized it didn't take much for me to lower my standards—a handsome face, a gorgeous body, a charming smile. Was I really so shallow? Not shallow, I decided. Flattered. Flattered, even if a bit puzzled, by Alex's attention and admiration. But, after all, what harm could come of it? We were simply keeping each other company for a while.

I finished my coffee and decided to go back to my room, sticking the paperback mystery I'd been reading into my canvas bag. I slipped on the rubber "Aloha Maui" sandals I'd bought at the hotel gift shop. Alex had left his beach bag behind. Since I didn't think it should be left unguarded, I decided to take it either to the registration desk or to his room.

Whistling softly, I followed one of several meandering paths up to the hotel, enjoying the elaborate artifice that had transformed sand dunes into a tropical jungle. Swaying date-nut palms, odd spike-leafed hala trees, six-foot-tall ferns, fruit-dangling papaya and avocado trees, exuberantly blossoming hibiscus bushes, and clusters of torch ginger and birds-of-paradise covered the gentle slope. The only thing missing was monkeys. And poisonous snakes.

A waterfall tumbled down from the lower level of the hotel over glistening black lava rocks, the white-foamed water subsiding, eventually, into pools filled with enormous orange and red and spotted carp. Neon-pink flamingos waded through side-streams of shallow water, and black swans preened themselves on an occasional oasis of bright green grass. Stone benches and Japanese archways played visual peek-a-boo as I strolled up the path. Birds called to each other, water spattered and hissed, and palm leaves rattled like tin cans in the breeze.

Contrary to general opinion, palm trees to do not rustle. They rattle. Loudly.

I stood still for a moment, breathed in the fragrant air, and smiled. For all my disappointment with Maui—it was too touristy, too lacking in native culture—and my distaste for so much greenery—I grew up in the Southwest and I'm just more comfortable with austerity—the hotel grounds were a constant source of pleasure. In the two days since I had arrived on Maui, I had already ambled through the garden several times, alone or with Alex, delighting in a newly discovered miniature gazebo, a flamingo balancing effortlessly on one leg, a languid gecko sunning on a rock.

The main path led to the hotel lobby; a path to the left, reached by crossing over a swinging bridge, led to the detached west wing of the hotel, where I was staying, and to a sunken Jacuzzi, partly screened by the dense foliage. A dip in a hot tub surrounded by ferns and hibiscus and gawking parrots sounded very appealing, so I turned off onto the narrow trail leading to the Jacuzzi, plunged through the vegetation, and reached the pool.

Floating face down on the surface, a body rotated gently, its limp limbs moving gracefully in the swirling water.

Two

The bronzed male back looked awfully familiar. I dropped the beach bag and ran to the hot tub, hoping it wasn't too late. Frantically, I pulled his arm towards me, then grabbed his head to lift his face out of the water.

My hands came away smeared with blood. Only then did I notice the foaming water was a murky red. Struggling against the swirling water and the strangely passive flesh, I managed to drag the body out of the tub and turn it over.

It was Alex. Golden-haired, golden-tongued Alex, his head caved in, blood dribbling down his face and puddling on the soft green grass. I suppose I should have screamed, but I was in shock. It was obvious he was dead, so I left him dripping on the lawn and raced back for help.

I ran up to the poolside bar and gasped, "There's a dead man in the Jacuzzi!"

The bartender reached for the phone and called security. From the look he gave me, I wasn't sure if he was calling security for the dead man or for me. The chattering guests who had been lounging nearby moved rapidly, soundlessly, away.

After a moment's hesitation, the bartender sloshed some bourbon in a glass and thrust it across the counter at me. I grabbed it and then, much to my surprise, my legs folded up under me.

It wasn't as if this was the first dead body I had seen. A few years earlier I had been standing right next to a man when he was fatally stabbed in the back. (See *Dead End on the Camino*.) But since the murdered man had been planning to kill me—and would have if someone hadn't killed him first—my sympathy for him was minimal. Alex, on the other hand, had been a charming companion, and even though I had only known him a few days, it was a shock to find his dead body floating in a hot tub.

Not just dead. Murdered. Why else was his head bashed in?

I took a large gulp of bourbon. I choked. When I quit sputtering I struggled to stand up. No longer immobilized by shock or, perhaps, ambivalence, the bartender deserted the haven of his bar, helped me stand, and led me to a nearby lounge chair.

Still slightly dazed, I looked around. The other guests had retreated to a safe distance, forming an isolation zone of empty chairs around me. It reminded me of the "kill" zone on a Petri dish. They pointedly refused to look at me directly, but I noticed sidelong glances. It was probably just as well. My long auburn hair had come undone from its twist and hung down in unkempt strands; my white shorts and T-shirt, my hands and legs, were splotched with blood.

I finished the drink, which didn't take any time at all, just as two hotel security guards approached. I could tell they were security by the appliquéd patches on the sleeves of their matching flower-printed Aloha shirts and by their matching walkie-talkies.

"What seems to be the problem?" the older one asked.

"I found a dead body in the Jacuzzi," I replied shakily.

They exchanged glances. The younger one ran up the path, the other walked over to the bar and made a phone call. Probably to the police, I thought.

Then he returned and sat down on the lounge chair next to me, close enough to grab me if I did something strange, far enough away so as not to be at risk.

I was an innocent bystander—at least I knew I was innocent—who had had the misfortune to discover a dead body. But rather than being comforted and commiserated, I was being treated as if I was contagious. Contagious and possibly dangerous.

We waited in silence. Soon two uniformed policemen approached. One was bulky, pock-marked, dark skinned; the other was skinny and pale faced. Mutt and Jeff. Actually, they were Larry Nakamura and Nestor Mendoza, as I learned during my subsequent lengthy, unpleasant interrogation.

It's hard to recall in detail what happened next. I remember they asked me to repeat what had happened and then to show them where I found the body. I did. The man from hotel security was standing guard. Alex was still lying there exactly as I had left him, which was not surprising, of course, since he was dead. The bourbon stirred uneasily in my stomach. I didn't want to look at the blood matted in his hair, but I found I couldn't look away. Unexpectedly, I started to cry.

Larry handed me a Kleenex. Nestor asked, "Anyone you know?"

I nodded. "Alex. Alex James Cook. He's staying at the hotel."

Nestor glanced at Larry, then inquired, "When did you last see him?"

"About half an hour ago. I was sitting on a lounge chair near the pool. He'd been snorkeling. He came up to me and we started talking. Then he left suddenly. After a while, I decided to go back to my room."

"Isn't the Jacuzzi a little off the beaten track?"

"I suppose, but I felt like a dip in the hot tub."

Nestor looked at my blood-stained shorts and shirt. "Where's your swimsuit?"

"Oh," I said, noticing my clothes in surprise. "I hadn't thought about that. The Jacuzzi was just a whim."

"Known him long?" he probed.

"I met him a few days ago. Thursday. When I first arrived at the hotel." I closed my eyes. It seemed like a lifetime ago.

Nestor nodded thoughtfully, then bent down to examine the body, turning it over gently. Since it no longer mattered to Alex whether Nestor was gentle or not, I suppose he was simply trying to avoid destroying evidence. He found a room key in a Velcroed pocket. Nothing else. Larry and the security guard scoured the grass around the Jacuzzi, presumably looking for the murder weapon. I say presumably, since they didn't tell me anything. They conferred for a few minutes over Alex's body. Then Larry came over, looked at me sadly, and read me my rights. A mere formality, Nestor assured me. I waived my rights, bewildered.

They took me in for questioning.

Larry and Nestor played off against each other. Maybe they switched roles on alternative days. Maybe not. At any rate, on that particular Saturday Larry was warm, friendly, considerate, and Nestor was everything Larry wasn't. As the morning wore on, I wore out. So did my patience.

The interview went something like the following.

Nestor, tight-lipped and pacing; Larry, smiling reassuringly and fiddling with the digital recorder.

Nestor: "You say you knew the dead man?"

"Yes. His name was Alex. Alex James Cook."

"Where did you meet him?"

"At the Trade Winds Bar at the Maui Surf."

"When?"

"Thursday afternoon."

It seemed much longer ago, of course. That's what vacations—and death—do to one's sense of time. My mind went back to my arrival on the island.

My plane had landed late in Honolulu, so I had missed my connection to Maui and had to wait half an hour for the next shuttle. I had arrived at Kahului Airport around 4 p.m. and gone directly to the nearby rental-car office to pick up a turquoise Sunbird convertible. A bit extravagant, I know, but you only live once.

Maui is shaped like a reclining bowling pin; the two mountain-filled loops are joined—or separated, depending on your point of view—by a narrow volcanic isthmus. I had driven south across the flat isthmus, admiring the jagged moss-green West Maui Mountains that form the smaller western loop and cloud-shrouded Haleakala, the 12,000-foot-high dormant volcano that forms the large eastern loop, and then continued driving south along the coast, pulling off at scenic spots and taking photos with my compact zoom camera. It was my first trip to a tropical island and I planned to make the most of it.

When I arrived at the Maui Surf Hotel, a valet parked my car and a bellboy grabbed my slightly shabby bag. Much to his disappointment, I wouldn't let him carry my briefcase. I followed him through the massive bronze-embellished glass doors that stood open, framing the entrance to the lobby.

It took me a moment to spot the reception desk. It was nearly hidden by a vast jungle filled with tropical trees and flowers, penguins waddling around a shaded pool (don't ask me what penguins were doing there), trained parrots preening themselves on pedestals, huge bronze statues—and that was just the main lobby. There was no back wall, so I could see straight through to the impossibly blue sky and a patch of equally impossibly green lawn at the far end.

The conference brochure had described the hotel as a full-service luxury Hawaiian resort, but I had been astounded at the cost: after all, what hotel room could be worth that much money? My skepticism faded rapidly. The bellhop cleared his throat and pointed towards to reception desk, and I checked in. When I got to my room, the bellhop was waiting to take me on a tour of the amenities: stocked refrigerator, stocked pantry filled with an assortment of macadamia-nut candies, the balcony (called a *lanai*, he informed me), the view. The room was furnished in elegant "island bamboo" style: a rattan sofa covered with bamboo-printed cushions, matching chairs, assorted rattan and glass tables, a pecan dresser, and a six-foot tall, hand-painted bamboo folding screen. Large, Japanese-style bird prints hung over the sofa; and a fragrant bouquet of yellow plumeria blossoms was artfully arranged in a large blue-and-gold cloisonné vase.

After tipping the bellhop—generously, I thought, but not generously enough, judging by his response—I quickly unpacked and then began exploring. I started with the lobby, taking time to admire the huge stone Buddha figures, life-size glazed ceramic horses, ornate carved vases, and inscribed bronze gongs, all very old and all discretely labeled with age and origin.

Then I wandered down wide corridors decorated with more museum-quality Asian art and lined with expensive shops, art galleries, restaurants, bars, and lounges. Several corridors opened directly onto the extensive tropical garden planted on the slope in back of the hotel. Or maybe it was the front of the hotel, since it faced the ocean.

The sound of music lured me back to the Trade Winds Bar, located in a tiny "unlandscaped" area near the registration desk. A pudgy, pony-tailed guitar player was singing songs from the seventies.

I curled up on a cushion-backed rattan sofa next to the low wall that divided the inside of the bar from outdoors. Tiny twittering birds flew in and out, perching momentarily amidst the flowers and greenery planted on top of the divider. A gentle breeze wafted in from the sea, bringing with it the sweet scent of plumeria blossoms. Ah, Paradise.

Nibbling on mixed nuts and pretzels, guaranteed to induce thirst, I studied the brightly colored drink menu and pondered which exotic fruit cocktail to try first. A waitress draped in a colorful, flower-strewn *pareau*—a kind of sarong—glided over to my table, her blond, waist-long hair held back with a silk hibiscus blossom. She gracefully handed me a drink the color of a pastel rainbow; a delicate orchid, a tiny paper parasol, and a fluted twist of orange peel perched on the rim of the hurricane-style glass. With a smile, she gestured towards a gorgeous blond hunk in white shorts and shirt, sitting at the bar. He lifted his matching glass and smiled. I smiled back.

That's how I met Alex.

"Miss Webster?"

With a start, I realized that Nestor was staring at me and Larry was drumming his fingers on the desk. They had been waiting for me to begin.

"I met Alex at the Trade Winds Bar here at the hotel. I'd just arrived, and I went to the bar to have a drink."

"So he picked you up, huh?"

In my best professorial tone, I said, "We met each other. We were both alone. It's much more fun to do things with somebody, don't you think?" I replied ingenuously.

Nestor had a cynical sneer pasted on his face. "My my, you make friends easy, don't you?"

I bridled. "I thought that was the idea. After all, the tourist brochures rave about the friendly "Aloha" spirit of Hawaii. I guess they didn't mean the police!"

Larry said calmly, "Now Miss Webster, it is Miss Webster, isn't it?"

I considered "Ms." but decided to "go for broke"—"Actually, it's Doctor. Dr. Noa Webster. I'm an associate professor of anthropology at a New York state college."

Nestor snorted and Larry nodded encouragingly. "And then? After you two met, what did you do?"

"We went to dinner at Trifles"—a thoroughly misleading name since it was the most expensive restaurant in the hotel—"And danced until midnight to live music in one of the hotel bars."

"And after dinner and drinking and dancing, what did you do?" Nestor demanded.

"I don't think that's any of your business," I replied coldly, then realized it might be some of his business after all, if it had some bearing on who killed Alex. "If you must know, I went to bed."

"And Alex?"

"He went to bed, too. At least I think he did."

"Together?" Nestor smirked.

"Hardly! Look, I don't know who you usually interrogate, but you've got the wrong idea. We enjoyed each other's company. Period."

"So you say."

Larry interrupted. "Where did you go dancing?"

"I don't remember. I could find out, I suppose. I saved the souvenir matchbox. It was black and gold, and the matches were unusual. Wax, I think."

"So you had a good time together and said goodnight at the door. I can believe that," Larry said, soothingly. "And the next day?"

"The next day, Friday, we took an all-day group tour of Hana Road, including a hike in the rain forest, a swim in the Seven Pools, and a visit to Lindbergh's grave. That evening we ate dinner at Aloha."

"That's that classy restaurant at the Royal Princess Resort?" Nestor asked.

"Right. It's next door to the Maui Surf, so we walked over along the beach, had dinner, drank Mai Tais and Maui Wowies, and watched the Polynesian dance review from the restaurant balcony."

"And what else did you do?" Larry continued.

"We talked. Alex told me all about himself. I told him all about myself."

"What did he tell you?"

"He said he was a tennis pro from California. He said was on Maui recovering from a broken heart."

Nestor snorted again. Maybe it was allergies. "And what are you doing on Maui, Miss Webster? Recovering from a broken heart, too?"

I ignored him and directed my reply to Larry. "I came here to present a paper at a conference on religious revitalization movements. The conference is being held at the Maui Surf."

"When's it start?" Nestor asked suspiciously.

"Thursday."

"Today's Saturday. You came Thursday. Why'd'ja come so early?"

"I came early so I could see some of this beautiful island before the conference."

"What's the paper about?" Larry asked.

"It's on medieval military orders in contemporary society."

"Military orders?" Nestor probed. "You been studying martial arts?"

"Nestor, give the lady a break!" Larry replied impatiently.

I was getting increasingly irritated. "I don't get it. Why aren't you looking for the murderer instead of giving me a hard time?"

"What makes you think it was a murder?" Nestor retorted.

I looked at him in disbelief. "Any idiot could tell that Alex didn't smash his head in by accident. And even if he had, why would he have climbed into the Jacuzzi to drown?"

Larry interjected, "We're not sure how he died. The coroner's report isn't back."

"It wasn't an accident," I insisted. "It was murder."

"You seem awful easy with murder talk, little lady," Nestor growled. "How come you aren't more upset?"

I sighed in disgust. Just then, someone tapped on the office window. Nestor left the room, closing the door behind him. Larry poured me a glass of water from the pitcher on the desk. I drank the tepid, stale liquid in silence.

After a few minutes, Nestor returned. "Why don't you quit lying and admit you were Alex's girlfriend?"

"What?" I sputtered.

Nestor repeated, gloating, "We know you're Alex's girlfriend and came to meet him. You've been wasting our time."

Taking a deep breath, I said, "The fact that I found him attractive doesn't mean I'm his girlfriend. Or hadn't that occurred to you—"

Larry stepped between us. "Now calm down, both of you."

Nestor continued, "Alex's real name is Alexander Bainbridge, not Alex James Cook. I thought that sounded suspicious. You think I'm dumb, but I know who discovered the Hawaiian Islands. We found Alexander's ID in his room. He's the son of one of the wealthiest old families in Oahu."

"He told me he was Alex James Cook and he lived in California!"

"So you say."

"Was he a tennis pro, at least?"

Nestor shook his head. "Not him. He had so much money he didn't have to work. A big house with a view of Diamond Head, a fancy yacht. Had a lot of money. And he spent it, too. He could buy whatever he wanted."

I thought I heard a note of bitterness. Well, why not? Nestor probably didn't earn much as a policeman. My mind wandered: was this an indication of class tension in Paradise? I found I preferred thinking about anything other than Alex's deception. And his death.

Larry was talking to Nestor. "Didn't you tell me Alex was an art collector or something?"

"Yeah, something like that." He turned on me. "Everybody knows you was his girlfriend. He mentioned you to the cleaning lady, the desk clerk, the bell boy—"

Everything I thought I'd known about Alex was wrong. Including his name. He'd lied not just to me, he'd lied to everyone. And he'd even lied about me. This should teach me to be friendly with strangers, especially attractive ones, I thought gloomily.

It had occurred to me to wonder why he was so attentive, but I really hadn't spent much time wondering. I was too busy being flattered. Now I started wondering. Not that I'm not. Attractive, that is. Or so I've been told by a few, make that a few too many, men. So why shouldn't men, even a somewhat younger man like Alex, want to spend time with me? Why indeed?

My mother always said I was too gullible. I guess she was right. I took a few deep breaths, trying to release the tension compressing my chest. In for five, out for five; in for five, out for five.

Nestor loomed over me. "Come on, Miss Webster, quit wasting my time. We know you're his girlfriend."

"If I were his girlfriend," I retorted, "Why were we staying in separate rooms?"

Nestor was taken aback. He paused a moment, then replied, "Just cause you registered separately doesn't mean you slept separate, now, does it?"

"Give me a break," I protested.

"Not likely!" Nestor growled.

My continued protests only drew a disbelieving smirk from Nestor. I told them my boyfriend Peter (actually, my on-again off-again boyfriend, but I didn't want to go into the murky details) was scheduled to join me at the end of the conference. No, they couldn't contact him, at least not easily. He was visiting relatives in England. Nestor and Larry looked at each other: a likely story.

"Let's start over, shall we?" Nestor said grimly.

I repeated the same story, but this time I remembered that I had been carrying Alex's beach bag when I discovered his body and that I'd left the bag behind when I ran for help. It wasn't there when we returned.

"Maybe the security man picked it up," I suggested.

Nestor shook his head.

"Who could have taken it?" I asked.

"Why didn't you remember earlier?" He countered.

"Somehow, it slipped my mind," I snarled, "I suppose from the shock of finding my friend floating face down in the Jacuzzi."

"Yeah, so you say."

Nestor and I glared at each other.

Larry asked, "Did Alex mention any names to you?"

"Names?"

"You know," he repeated patiently. "Names. People."

"Not to me."

"Nobody at all? Think hard."

My thinking was growing increasingly torpid. With an effort, I recalled something. "Alex said he was going to look up an old friend, a banker, I think, or maybe he was an investment counselor."

Nestor pounced. "What was his name?"

"Al something," I said hesitantly.

"Something?" Larry asked gently.

"The last name was Hawaiian. At least I think it was, since it sounded so unusual."

Nestor just looked at me, smiling nastily, and told me to begin again. This time I rebelled. I was furious with his attitude and, besides,

I was starving. It was long past lunchtime, and my blood sugar was sinking fast.

"Look," I said as calmly as I could, "I'm willing to cooperate but I resent your bullying. After all, I'm just an innocent witness—and not even to murder, since all I did was discover the dead body. If you insist on treating me as a suspect, I'll call a lawyer."

I waited, shaky from anger, nerves, and hunger, while they debated what to do. Larry won. Since I wasn't being charged with anything, at least not yet, they agreed to let me go. I picked up my bag and stood up. I felt a little woozy.

Larry drove me back to the hotel in silence. When we arrived, he said apologetically, "Sorry about Nestor. His girlfriend left him a few months ago. He still isn't over it."

"I don't think I blame her," I grumbled.

"I sure don't want this to ruin your visit to Maui, Dr. Webster," he said apologetically. "Try to have a good time, but be careful. Very careful." He handed me his card and opened the door. "If anything unusual happens, let me know. Try my cell phone, but it may not work. Coverage is real spotty on the island. Which reminds me, what's your cell phone number?"

"I didn't bring my cell phone. I was on vacation, remember?"

"Right. Sorry, Doctor. Merry Christmas, okay? *Mele Kalikimaka.*"

"Merry Christmas to you, too," I said wearily.

I got out of the car and walked away, his words echoing in my head—"Be careful. Very careful. If anything unusual happens, let me know." Like what, I wondered. Another dead body? And whose would it be this time? Mine?

Three

I ignored the look the doorman gave me as I stomped into the lobby, but was it my imagination, or did people seem to move away as I approached? Suddenly I realized I was still wearing the bourbon-drenched, blood-stained clothes I had had on that morning. No wonder they avoided me. Quickly, I located a nearby exit, walked briskly past a pair of squawking parrots, and ran up the path to the west wing, then up the stairs to the third floor.

Panting slightly, I stood on the walkway that overlooked the central atrium and fumbled with my room key. The minute I opened the door, I knew someone had been there. I am not a tidy person, but I could tell. Even in apparent chaos there can be order. The sandals I had tossed off randomly the night before were now lined up side by side, and the clothes I had strewn on the chair had been rearranged: my underpants—the last thing I habitually take off—were no longer on top.

The tourist brochures I had piled on the glass-topped rattan table also seemed to have been disturbed, but I couldn't be sure. Nervously,

I checked my briefcase. Yes, the paper I was to present a week from Sunday was still there. Whoever had searched the room hadn't taken anything. Not that there was anything to take.

Reaching for the phone, I dialed the number on the card Larry had given me. Nestor answered.

"Yeah? Mendoza here."

"Oh," I said, disappointed. "I want to talk to Larry."

"Not here." Pause. "Miss Webster?"

Grudgingly, I muttered, "Right."

"So you want to make a statement?"

"Hardly. I decided to report that someone has searched my room."

"So? We had a search warrant."

"Oh."

"By the way, Miss Webster, it's no use pretending you just met Alex."

"Why do you keep insisting I'm lying?"

"We found two tickets to Hong Kong in his dresser."

"So?" I said, puzzled.

"Yeah. To Hong Kong. Leaving this evening."

"This evening?"

"Made out to Mr. and Mrs. Alexander Bainbridge."

"You mean he was married?" I said, in surprise.

"Not that we know of."

"Well, I assure you, he didn't invite me to go to Hong Kong. Besides, I'm giving a paper Friday at the conference."

"Come'on, Miss Webster, let's quit playing games."

"Believe me, if I knew anything I'd tell you. I want to catch his murderer as much as you do."

"Yeah, sure."

"Look, Mr. Mendoza—"

"No, you look," he interrupted. "I don't know what your game is, but I'm gonna find out. In the meantime, don't leave the island. Don't do anything stupid—"

"Like expecting the police to be helpful!" I slammed the phone down, seething, then called room service. They promised to bring lunch in half an hour. To tide me over, I took a small can of crunchy macadamia-nut brittle from the pantry and started nibbling. I could practically feel the sugar hit my bloodstream. Then I stripped off my clothes and headed for the shower.

Fifteen minutes later, wet hair wrapped in a huge Turkish towel, body wrapped in a silky, orchid-patterned *pareau*, I searched through my bag for the nail polish I had bought the day before. As I rummaged through the jumbled contents, my fingers encountered something rough and oddly shaped. Recoiling, I withdrew my hand and tossed the contents onto the bed. A small dark object emerged.

It was Alex's *tiki* doll.

With a shiver, I picked it up. Its glittering green eyes glared back at me. Puzzled and disturbed by this unexpected souvenir, I propped it up on the dresser and stared at it. I was sure I had given the *tiki* back to Alex, so how had it gotten into my purse? And why? Although I had a possible answer to "how," I had not the slightest idea of "why."

Staring at the crude, vaguely menacing carving proved unenlightening, so I began painting my toenails a color called "Hawaiian Sunset"—I had bought the polish at the hotel gift shop the day before. For some obscure reason, painting my toenails made me feel better able to face the rest of the day.

Just as I completed the last toenail and several mental recyclings of the morning events, I heard a timid knock on the door.

"Who is it?"

A muffled voice replied.

Trying not to smear my polish, I waddled over to the door and peered through the peephole. Standing on the other side was an old Hawaiian man wearing a straw hat, his wrinkled face slightly distorted by the peephole. He didn't look like room service.

"What do you want?" I asked through the door.

"Please, I need to talk with you," he replied in an oddly lilting, slightly accented voice.

"About what?" I asked suspiciously.

"About my *mo'opuna*, my granddaughter."

"Your granddaughter?"

"Yes. She was dating your friend Alex."

Alex had never mentioned a Hawaiian girlfriend, but Alex had not mentioned a lot of things. Besides, as I had already discovered, much of what he had said had been lies.

My visitor looked harmless enough, and I was intrigued, so I opened the door. Standing in front of me was a large, heavy-set man wearing a beat-up straw hat, a faded Aloha shirt, baggy khaki pants, and worn, rubber *zoris* on his broad brown feet. A necklace of polished chocolate-brown *kukui* nuts hung around his neck. His face was square, his eyes large, his nose thick and broad. His skin was the color of dark-roasted cashew nuts. He looked Polynesian, not Asian, a subtle difference explained by the tour guide the day before, but hard to describe.

He stood there nervously for a moment, shifting his weight from one foot to the other, then took off his hat. His cropped, slightly curly hair was steel gray.

"Can I come in?" he asked.

I moved back and he entered the room, leaving the door open behind him. We stood looking at each other for a moment, separated by the width of the door and by the swath of light streaming in from the atrium.

I waited for him to begin.

Twisting his hat in his hands, he said, "My name is David Kukuilani. My granddaughter, Melemele Kaohu, is—was—the girl-friend of Alexander Bainbridge."

I waited.

"I heard about the murder on the radio and came to help my granddaughter. But I can't find her."

"You can't find her?" I asked.

He shook his head. "I think she is with friends. I hope so, but I am worried."

"Why are you asking me for help?"

Hesitantly, he explained, "I heard them talk in the hotel. They say you found the body. And they say you are his girlfriend." He looked at me. "But she was his girlfriend. So I am puzzled."

I sympathized. "So am I."

His eyes moved cautiously around the room and came to rest on the *tiki* doll. As if mesmerized, he strode over to the dresser and picked it up, holding it reverently in his hands. Then he turned abruptly and demanded, "Where did you get this?"

Startled, I replied, "Alex had it."

"Alex had it?" he repeated.

"Yes. He was playing with it."

He ignored me as he contemplated the crude wooden figure.

"Alex said it was just a souvenir," I observed, "but somehow I didn't believe him."

He nodded solemnly. "It is good you do not let appearances de-ceive you." He glanced at me. "You have heard about the robbery?"

"What robbery?" I asked, bewildered.

"Several days ago—Wednesday—somebody robbed the Hawaiian Culture Museum in Wahaliu."

"Wahaliu? Is that on Maui?"

"No, on Oahu. They took four small wooden carvings." He paused. "This is one of them."

"What is it?" I asked.

"It is one of four sacred figures of the Hawaiian gods Ku, Kanaloa, Lono, and Kane. They belonged to King Kamehameha the Great."

"How can you be sure this is one of the figures?"

"I have seen them many times. I am sure."

Looking at the crude wooden carving, I asked, "Why would they be worth stealing?"

He paused a moment, then said, "The newspaper says they are worth a million dollars."

"You mean this little figure is worth $250,000?" I gasped.

"This is the least valuable, but it is still worth $150,000 or so."

"Do the others look like this?"

"They are all different because they are different gods. This one is smallest. The largest is almost six inches long."

I reached for the wooden carving; reluctantly, he gave it to me.

"It doesn't look valuable," I said, turning it over in my hands.

"The newspaper said the eyes are emeralds, and the earrings are black pearls."

"But surely that doesn't add up to $150,000."

"The carvings are very rare. And old. Almost 200 years old."

Two hundred years doesn't sound very old, I know, but in a tropical country where organic material rots quickly, it is actually quite ancient. And the connection with the legendary king who had united the Hawaiian islands obviously made the carvings even more valuable. Actually, beyond value. Irreplaceable.

My visitor continued fiercely, "But their true value cannot be measured in dollars. Their true value is to us, the Hawaiian people. They are our last link with our ancestors. By right, they belong to us!"

"Who's 'us'?" I asked, staring uneasily at this strange intruder who looked like an illiterate peasant but spoke with such surprising knowledge and authority. "And who are you?"

Seeming to grow in height and breadth, he declared, "I am a *kahuna*, a Hawaiian priest. For years, we had been trying to get the museum to return the *tikis* to us, but they have refused. Now it is too late. They have been stolen."

I nodded thoughtfully, remembering the movement to return religious objects to the American Indian tribes from whom they had been stolen or "purchased," and the UNESCO[1] ruling against transportation of sacred objects out of their country of origin. The legal—and moral—issues were complex. After all, some of these items were received as gifts. Or bought in good faith. And carefully preserved and lovingly displayed. Many of the traditions have been lost, or the practitioners have died out. So who is the rightful custodian today? And how do you right an ancient wrong?

"Where did you get this?" He demanded again, pointing at the figure in my hand.

"I told you, Alex had it. He must have given it to me."

He looked at me with obvious disbelief.

Startled, I replied, "Surely you don't think I had anything to do with the robbery? I didn't even arrive in Hawaii until Thursday!"

There was a knock on the door. Room service had arrived. The old Hawaiian priest unobtrusively disappeared behind the door and the bellhop wheeled in a bamboo and glass cart.

---

[1] *United Nations Educational, Scientific and Cultural Organization*

Smiling, the bellhop asked, "Would you like lunch on the *lanai*?"

I nodded absent-mindedly, then followed him out to the balcony. With a flourish, he removed the silver dome from a large service tray and set the table. I signed the bill, a bit stunned at the cost of a breaded *mahi-mahi* sandwich and French fries. You'd think local fish would be inexpensive, but Maui was full of surprises.

As soon as the bellhop left, the *kahuna* stepped forward onto the *lanai*. I looked at him warily from across the table.

"Perhaps we can help each other," he began.

"Look, Mr.—what did you say your name is?"

"Call me David. David Kukuilani."

"David Kukuilani," I repeated, trying to remember the name. I'm terrible at names, even when I'm not starved and stressed out because of the violent death of a new friend.

"Look, David. I'm hungry and I want to eat. It's been a very difficult day. Could you come back later?"

Solemnly, he said, "Later may be too late."

With a sigh, I said, "Okay. You talk while I eat."

Four

I placed the figure in the middle of the table and began to eat. The sandwich was soggy and the French fries were cold, but I was so hungry it didn't matter. Between bites, I queried David.

"Let me see if I have this right. Your granddaughter, Mele—"

"Melemele Kaohu. She is named for the sacred Hawaiian songs. Melemele means 'chant-chant.'"

"Your granddaughter Melemele was Alex's girlfriend."

"Yes."

"So why does everybody think I'm his girlfriend?" I asked, remembering the unpleasant exchange I had had with Mendoza.

David shook his head, puzzled. "I have asked in the hotel, and Alex told them. But I don't know why he lied."

"At least you believe I'm not his girlfriend."

"Of course I believe you," he paused, then continued slowly, "but I don't know who you are."

"Oh. Of course. I'm Noa Webster." We shook hands. His hand felt warm and dry; his grip was powerful.

"Noa Webster . . . ." He looked at me quizzically. "Your first name is Polynesian?"

I laughed. "Most people think it's biblical, but you're right. I was named for Gauguin's autobiography, Noa Noa."

"The name means 'sweet sweet fragrance'," he said with a smile, then added, in a serious tone, "I still don't understand why you have the sacred carving."

"Me neither."

"Perhaps you know something you aren't telling me," he said, looking me in the eyes. It was an unsettling experience and, even though I was hiding nothing, I looked away.

"Why do you say that?" I asked, thinking as I said it that there were a number of reasons why I might not tell him everything.

"Maybe you are an art dealer?"

"No, I'm an anthropologist."

"Ah, then that explains it."

"Explains what?" I asked, puzzled.

"How you knew that the carving was 'real.' I thought maybe you were an art dealer. They can usually tell about these things because of what they know."

"I'm an anthropologist; I know nothing about Hawaiian art. But the carving reminded me of a kachina doll."

"Kachina doll?"

"It's a misnomer, actually. They're not really dolls. They're made by the Native Americans who live in the southwestern United States. They represent the various Hopi spirits or gods and are quite sacred.

The 'real' ones are, that is. Of course, they're very popular with tourists, so the stores are full of copies made for souvenirs."

He nodded. "Just like the *tikis*."

"Right. Just like the *tikis*. And just like this *tiki*, you can tell the difference between a real one and a souvenir. I don't know how to explain it. It's not the fineness of the carving. Or the details. It's something else."

He nodded slowly. "You must not let appearances deceive you." Still staring at the figure, he changed the subject. "I am worried about my granddaughter. I hope she is not in trouble."

I ventured, "Would she have had any reason to kill Alex?"

He shook his head. "No reason. My granddaughter would not kill anyone. Besides, she told me a few days ago that they were going to get engaged."

"Just a thought," I said. After all, somebody had had a reason to kill Alex. Maybe she had been jilted—but apparently not, if they were going to get engaged.

I continued eating in silence, mulling over what he had, or had not, told me. Could his granddaughter have witnessed the murder? Not likely. Alex had only been gone for a few minutes. But why had he rushed off so abruptly? Had he suddenly remembered an appointment? With her? Maybe she was the "Mrs. Bainbridge" on the airline ticket. Then again, maybe not.

The *kahuna* was staring at the ocean, and I turned to look. Wind surfers, their many-colored sails resembling a flock of butterflies, glided over the rippling sea. A large outrigger canoe came into view.

"What's that?" I asked, pointing at the canoe.

"It is a modern copy of an ancient Hawaiian war canoe. They are preparing for the *luau* at the Royal Princess. My granddaughter is one of the hula dancers in the review. She comes riding in on the canoe, and then she and a group of warriors land on the beach in front of the hotel."

"Sounds like quite a spectacle."

"I have never seen it, but my granddaughter has told me about it. She wants me to see it, but I don't like this tourism and what it does...."

The canoe abruptly disappeared around a jagged volcanic outcropping. I finished lunch and pushed the plate away, then leaned forward in my chair.

"You said maybe we could help each other. Just what did you have in mind?"

"I am looking for my *mo'opuna*, my granddaughter."

"And?"

"And you are suspected of murdering Alex. Perhaps together we can find out who killed him."

"Now wait a minute!" I protested. "Nobody's accused me of anything!"

He smiled grimly. "They will."

He might be right at that, I thought. "I don't see how I can help you find your granddaughter. Or help find Alex's murderer."

His eyes, like mine, returned to the carved figure in the middle of the table. "You have one of the sacred *tikis*. That must be a clue."

"That's true," I admitted, "but I don't know why I have it. Or how I got it. Or where the others are. Besides, isn't this a matter for the police?"

The *kahuna* shifted a bit in his chair and stared out to sea again. Then he spread his gnarled hands helplessly. "You are an anthropologist. You must understand. There is so little we can do, my people and I, to keep our traditions alive. We have tried. I practice the old religion. My granddaughter dances the sacred hula dances. But that is not enough." His voice rose fiercely. "If we find the *tikis*, perhaps we will learn who murdered Alex. The *tikis* must be found! They must be returned to my people! Only you can help me!"

My sympathies—anthropological and emotional—were aroused, as he knew they would be. I did want to help, but that impulse had gotten me into trouble before. Trying to be reasonable, I asked, "Why not go to the police for help?"

There was a knock on the door.

"I'll see who's there," I said, and went back into the room, leaving David alone on the *lanai*.

It was Larry Nakamura and Nestor Mendoza.

"Speak of the devil," I muttered.

"May we come in?" Larry asked.

"Why bother to ask?" I replied. "Or don't you have a search warrant this time?"

Nestor looked at me menacingly. "Watch out, little lady."

Angrily, I said, "Look, I haven't done anything and I've already told you everything I know."

"Yeah. So you say," Nestor growled.

"Couldn't you leave him somewhere? Like in a kennel?" I asked Larry.

"Nestor, I thought we agreed—" Larry said, frustrated, then turned back to me. "Sorry, Dr. Webster. We have some questions to ask you."

"And I have some questions to ask you! Why did you search my room?"

"Standard procedure, Ma'am."

"I doubt it."

"Going native, are we?" Nestor leered.

Suddenly I realized I was still wearing the flower-strewn *pareau*. With David I had felt perfectly natural. With Nestor, I felt slightly indecent. A three-piece suit would probably have felt indecent, with Nestor.

With a sigh, I said, "Just a minute. Let me change."

Before they could protest, I slammed the door shut. When I turned back into the room, I realized with a shock that David was no longer on the balcony. I ran out to the *lanai*, but he was gone. My room was on the third floor, and he could not have leaped or climbed over to another *lanai*—the distance was too great. For a moment I wondered if he had paranormal powers that enabled him to disappear, but I instantly rejected that.

The police started knocking impatiently, so I quickly put on a T-shirt and shorts, then opened the door and gestured for them to come in.

"As you can see," I said, pointing at the empty *lanai*, "I was just finishing lunch. What can I do for you?"

"Just wondered if you've thought of anything you forgot to tell us this morning, like maybe the name of Alex's friend?" Larry asked.

"I've tried, but I haven't thought of anything."

"Try again," Nestor snarled.

Ignoring him, I asked Larry, "Have you found out anything?"

"Nothing Nestor didn't tell you earlier. Except that we checked out your credentials, and they seem okay."

"But you searched my room. Does this mean I'm still a suspect?" I asked suspiciously.

Nestor looked pleased. "You might say that. After all, you were there at the scene of the crime."

"Nobody's found Alex's black beach bag?"

"If there was one," Nestor replied. "We only have your word for it."

Larry added, "Not that we don't believe you, of course."

"Of course," I said sarcastically. Glancing at the now-empty terrace, I decided to tell them about the *tiki*. "Do you know anything about a recent museum robbery?"

Larry and Nestor exchanged glances. "Like what?" Larry asked.

"Well, somebody told me there was a robbery at the Hawaiian Culture Museum a few days ago. I just wondered if there might be a connection."

"And just what do you know about that?" Nestor snarled.

Larry interrupted, "Why do you think there might be a connection?"

"I know this is going to sound strange," I said hesitantly, "but after I left the police station I found a little *tiki* doll in my purse, and I think it might be one of the ones stolen from the museum."

"In your purse?" Nestor turned to Larry with a gloating smile.

I began to wish I hadn't been so forthcoming.

"And just how did you get this 'little *tiki* doll'?" Nestor asked.

My voice slightly hoarse—it gets hoarse when I'm nervous—I replied, "I'm not sure. I think Alex must have slipped it in my purse when I wasn't looking. He'd been playing with it."

With a laugh, Nestor exclaimed, "How stupid do you think we are, lady! And just where is this 'little *tiki* figure' now?"

I walked over to the *lanai*. The figure was gone. Along with David.

"I don't know," I admitted. "It was here on the table a minute ago, but now it's gone. I had a visitor, a Hawaiian priest, but he's gone too."

Shaking his head, Nestor replied, "Lady, you are really full of it, aren't you. For a minute, I thought you were on to something."

"But—"

"But nothing!" Eyes narrowed, he continued, "Or maybe you do know something. But not what you're telling. We know you didn't arrive in Maui on your scheduled flight. Just what were you doing on Oahu?"

"If you know that much," I retorted, "you should know my flight from the mainland was delayed. I missed the shuttle and had to take another one."

Larry frowned. "Dr. Webster, this is serious business. If you know anything about Alex Bainbridge's involvement in the museum theft, you'd better tell us."

"We can always take you back in for questioning, remember."

Frustrated, I turned to Larry. "All I know is Alex had a small *tiki*. It showed up in my purse after he died. And today I had a visitor, a Hawaiian priest. His name was David, David something. I can't remember his last name."

Nestor snorted.

I plunged ahead. "He said the carving was one of the *tikis* from the museum. He also said his granddaughter was Alex's girlfriend."

Nestor startled and looked more interested.

"What's her name?" Larry asked.

"Melemele."

He waited expectantly, then asked gently, "Melemele what?"

Embarrassed, I said, "I don't remember."

"Good try," Nestor sneered.

"What?"

"Good try at throwing the suspicion onto someone else. Somebody like Alex's imaginary girlfriend."

Angry, I wished I had kept my mouth shut. Honesty was obviously not the best policy. Well, I had tried to do my proverbial duty as a law-abiding citizen. So much for that. Never again.

Larry took Nestor by the shoulder and turned him towards the door. "Dr. Webster, for your sake, I hope you're telling us everything you know."

"What difference does it make?" I said bitterly. "You don't believe me anyway!"

I slammed the door after them and, slightly shaky, went out to the *lanai*. Leaning on the metal railing, I stared at the distant green waves, foaming white as they broke with a roar against the golden sand. The colorful wind surfers were gone for the day, and the beach was deserted. David was gone, too, along with the *tiki*. It had been a mistake to trust him. And I couldn't trust the police because they didn't trust me. Whom could I trust?

Somebody made a noise, and I spun around. David was standing there in the room, holding the *tiki* in one hand.

Furious, I demanded, "Why did you disappear? And how?"

"I did not think it wise to be seen, so I hid behind the screen in the corner."

I glanced at the woven bamboo screen. In my hurry, I hadn't looked behind it. "Why did you take the *tiki*?"

"It must not fall into the wrong hands." He hesitated a moment, then gave it back to me. "You must take care of it. And you must help me find the others."

With an old-fashioned, dignified bow, he turned and walked out of the room.

I called after him, "Wait—"

He turned and smiled inscrutably. "You will see me again."

Five

I don't know how long I sat there on the terrace staring, mesmerized, at the waves; listening, hypnotized, to the repetitive crashing of the surf. But gradually another sound intruded—the twanging sound of the Hawaiian guitar. Male voices wafted up from the patio crooning "Blue Hawaii." I had always suspected Hawaiian music was only heard on the mainland, but they really do sing like that on Hawaii. It was 5 p.m., and the evening entertainment had begun.

Five o'clock. Almost my entire day had been spent dealing with Alex's death. Some vacation in paradise.

A rapidly strummed ukulele accompanied the singers in the "The Hawaiian Wedding Song." The lyrics, at least the ones I could make out, were naïve but refreshing. A welcome change. I decided to go watch the performance.

Twisting my long, still-damp hair into a bun, I secured it with an ornamental chopstick, then plucked a plumeria blossom from the vase and stuck it in my hair. Before leaving, I slipped the *tiki* back in my purse.

After locking the door I walked briskly down the corridor and three flights of steps to the garden path. As I approached the turn-off to the Jacuzzi, I felt a sudden chill. Maybe it was just the gentle island breeze.

A dozen tables had been set out on the patio near the bar. Facing the audience, their backs to the ocean and a cluster of palm trees, a trio of white-clad musicians perched on high bar stools. One played the Hawaiian guitar, one strummed a ukulele, the other plucked a bass. Two of them were singing lilting Hawaiian lyrics in falsetto. An acquired taste, I decided, not at all sure I wanted to acquire it.

I selected a small table toward one side, with a good view of the band and the sea. Soon a *pareau*-clad waitress drifted over and took my order—one Maui Wowie and a small *pupu* platter.

The rainbow-hued drink arrived, complete with orange slice, miniature orchid, tiny paper parasol, and memories. This was the drink Alex had bought me in the lobby bar just two days before. And now he was dead and I was under suspicion. After a silent toast, I took a long swallow of the fruity cocktail, then another. Then I contemplated the assorted appetizers. Soy-sauce coated chicken wings. Tiny barbecued pork ribs. Water chestnut and garlicky chicken livers on a bamboo skewer. Deep-fried shrimp chips that looked like colored plastic but tasted like shrimpy potato puffs. At this rate, I wouldn't need dinner.

Half of the tables were occupied. Next to me two blond, sunburned parents and look-alike sunburned girls were demolishing hamburgers and drinking cokes. The girls had on matching Hawaiian gecko T-shirts; the parents wore matching white polo shirts emblazoned with the crest of the Maui Surfside. While I watched, the kids started tossing French fries at each other. The parents ignored them.

At another table, two men were drinking beer and eating party mix from a basket. One of them had tried unsuccessfully to disguise his bald spot by parting his hair at ear level and combing long, greasy strands from the left side over the top to the right side. The breeze had ruffled his careful arrangement, and he was trying to pat it back in place. His companion had a full head of faded red hair, which he nervously brushed back from his freckled forehead. After a few minutes, the red-headed man stood up, hitched up his pants, and strode away. Soon the other man tossed some dollar bills on the table and followed.

Close by, a young couple sat side by side, holding hands, their faces turned to each other in mirrored expressions of adoration. Honeymooners, I decided. Or maybe not, I reconsidered. After all, nothing kills ardor as quickly as marriage. I ought to know, having tried it once.

A middle-aged man sat alone, drumming his fingers on the table. He was wearing a white, short-sleeved shirt and beige pants. His appearance was unremarkable: medium-short, medium-brown hair, regular features. No gold chains, no earrings. A gold-banded wristwatch, but too far away for me to see the brand. While I watched, he signaled the waitress to come over; after a brief discussion, she walked off but soon returned with a newspaper.

An elegantly coifed older woman dressed in yards of fluttering, hand-painted silk and lots of clinking gold bracelets sat alone at another table. Nervously, she played with the long string of pearls dangling around her neck. After a few minutes, a young, attractive man came over to her, kissed the nape of her neck, and sat down beside her. They began an animated, whispered conversation. Her son? Not likely.

At another table, a young woman was writing in a small black notebook. Huge shell earrings dangled from her ears, and her hair was cropped exceedingly short, a style that emphasized her high cheekbones and clear, translucent skin; maybe it was just the light, but her dark-rimmed eyes looked slightly bruised. Too many late nights? Jet lag?

She was wearing an oversized T-shirt, hand-painted with tropical fish, presumably purchased at the local swap meet. Surreptitiously, she glanced around the patio. Our eyes met, and she quickly looked away. What had she heard about me—or was I being paranoid? Perhaps she was just shy. And alone. And uncomfortable about being alone. Idly, I wondered if she also was attending the conference and had come early to enjoy Maui. If so, I hoped her vacation had been more enjoyable than mine.

A tall, bearded man in wrinkled khakis, garish Aloha shirt, and new Birkenstock sandals stood by the edge of the patio. With a start, I recognized him and waved. After a moment, he recognized me and came over to the table.

"Noa Webster, isn't it?" He said as he sat down.

"Right. Robert . . .."

"Wiley."

"Sorry," I apologized, "I'm really bad at names. Good at faces, bad at names."

"No problem. It's been a few years since we last met."

"At that pilgrimage conference in Spain, wasn't it?"

"Right."

"What brings you to Maui? Giving a paper?" I said, wishing I could remember the program schedule.

He nodded. "On Thursday. Opening day."

"Mine's on Friday."

"I noticed."

"So what brings you to the Maui Surfside a week early?" I asked. "A well-deserved vacation?"

"Oh, I'm not staying here. I just dropped by to see the sights. It's amusing to see how the other half—or is it 5%?—live. Actually, I'm staying with friends. I'm on Maui to finish a project."

"Fieldwork?"

He nodded. "I've been studying the revitalization of traditional Hawaiian religion, and there's an old *kahuna* on the island who's a fantastic informant."

"Old *kahuna*?" Hesitantly I asked, "By any chance, is his name David something?"

"David Kukuilani."

"So he really is a *kahuna*," I said aloud. Not that I had ever really doubted it.

Puzzled, Robert said, "One of the best. Do you know him?"

"Well," I hesitated, "I met him under rather mysterious circumstances."

"Tell me more," Robert said.

"It's a long story." While I searched for a pen to write down David's last name, I tried to decide how much of the story to tell. Very little, I determined. After all, it wouldn't do my professional reputation any good to have it widely known I was suspected of murder.

"To make it brief, he came to my room looking for information about his granddaughter. And he saw a *tiki* I had . . . .." I paused, then decided not to say anything more.

"They're close-knit, these native Hawaiians. They have large extended families and maintain strong kinship ties. If David's worried about his granddaughter, he would try to help her." Narrowing his eyes, he said, "You said a *tiki*?"

I nodded.

"He's a real expert on them. We spent a lot of time in the Culture Museum on Wahaliu, examining the collection. They've got—or rather had—some very significant *tikis*. Have you heard about the robbery?"

I nodded, eager to change the subject. "So you vouch for David, do you?"

"I'm not sure what you mean, but I suppose so," he said slowly. "David is a highly respected *kahuna*. You can take his word for things."

"Thanks. That's reassuring."

As an afterthought he added, "He's got a few bees in his bonnet, if you know what I mean, but he's 'the real *kahuna*.'" He laughed at his own joke.

I laughed with him, a bit uneasily. I'd never really thought before about what that phrase meant.

The band was playing "Blue Hawaii." The easy, swooping sound reminded me of the music they used to play in roller-skating rinks. Maybe they still do.

Grimacing, Robert stood up, scraping the chair on the cement. "I hate this kind of music. I'm leaving. Care to come along?"

I shook my head. "I'm tempted, believe me, but I've had a long day. I think I'll just stay here a while, soak up the atmosphere, and go to bed early."

"May I give you a call sometime?"

"Sure thing."

"By the way, if you see the *kahuna* again, tell him I'm looking for him. He's a hard man to get hold of."

"Will do."

With a smile, Robert said, "Aloha," and walked away.

The song ended and the leader stood up. Breathing heavily into the microphone, he announced, "Ladies and gentlemen, tonight we have a special treat for you. Our lovely island princess, our very special Maui maiden! Ladies and gentlemen, I want you to give a big welcome to Aloha!" With an expansive gesture, he motioned towards the palm trees nearby. He started to clap, and some of us joined in.

Out stepped a young woman dressed in a form-fitting, strapless, red-and-black flower-printed dress. Her black hair flowed like liquid jet down her back; a red hibiscus blossom was tucked behind one ear.

Aloha stood for a moment in front of the band, still as a reflecting pool. Then she began to dance. She was as graceful as a gently swaying palm tree, beautiful as a bouquet of fragrant frangipani. Even the kids at the table next to me stopped squabbling and watched.

Her mouth fixed in a shy smile, Aloha's dark eyes stared unfocussed at the audience. Absorbed in her dance, she interpreted the lyrics of the songs in fluid gestures. Knees slightly bent, hips swaying gently, her broad, bare feet moved in time with the music and the palm trees and the waves.

Pupus getting cold, drink getting warm, I watched, almost forgetting to breathe, captivated by Aloha's performance. Even though the hula she did was undoubtedly altered for tourists, it transported me to an era before the white man came, when the sacred hula was worship in motion, when the soul of Hawaii moved to the ancient rhythm of the sea and the stars, when the fire goddess Pele could be placated with an offering and the red-mouthed war god Kukailimoku could be appeased with blood.

Several songs and hulas later, the band stopped playing and the leader again stood up. With a start, I came out of my trance.

"We're going to take a break now, folks, and let our beautiful little Aloha rest. We'll be back in 15 minutes with a special surprise just for you, so don't go away!"

The musicians and the dancer walked off stage towards the hotel, following a sidewalk that led next to my table. As they passed by, I overheard a snatch of conversation between Aloha and the leader.

"Where the hell were you, Aloha? You were supposed to be here half an hour ago!"

She replied sullenly, "I got held up."

"Don't let it happen again!"

Even in sulky retreat, Aloha moved gracefully, her bare feet padding soundlessly on the cement trail.

I nibbled without tasting on a cold shrimp chip, pondering the difference between the enchanting stage persona and the moody, flat-voiced woman who had just passed by.

"Excuse me."

Startled, I looked up to see the nondescript man from the nearby table standing next to me.

"Yes?"

"Aren't you the woman who found the . . . ah . . . dead body this morning?"

Oh, God, I thought. A groupie. Or worse yet, a ghoulie.

Cautiously, I replied, "So what if I am?"

"Your boyfriend Alex."

"Not you, too!" I exclaimed, exasperated.

"I beg your pardon?"

I took a deep breath. It wasn't his fault that he had gotten the wrong impression. "You were right on the first guess, wrong on the second. I was his friend, not his girlfriend. I just met him a few days ago."

He paused for a moment, nonplussed, then said, "Oh. I see."

"What do you see?" I asked, annoyed.

He ignored me and continued, "I still think we have something in common."

"Like what?"

"A mutual interest."

"Such as?"

"Do you mind if I sit down?"

While I tried to decide how much I minded, he sat down.

With an engaging smile, he said, "I'm a friend of Alex's, too."

I waited for him to continue.

"I'm just as shocked as you are about what happened this morning. Why anyone would want to kill good old Alex . . .."

"You knew Alex?" I asked skeptically.

"Why, yes. We were friends. And business acquaintances, on a few occasions."

"Is your name Al, by any chance?" I asked.

"No, it's Bill. Bill Miller. Why?"

"Alex mentioned an old friend, someone named Al. I thought maybe . . .."

"Sorry. Not me. But if you tell me Al's last name, I might know him. I know several of Alex's friends."

Ruefully, I replied, "That's the problem. I don't remember."

"Well, perhaps you'll remember later," he said with a smile. "If you do, maybe I can help."

"Help what?"

"Help you get in touch with him."

"Why would I want to do that?"

"Perhaps you don't."

Puzzled, I replied, "I don't understand what you're getting at."

"My dear, I'm not getting at anything. Perhaps you wanted to notify him of Alex's death. Perhaps not. Forgive me."

"Just how well did you know Alex?" I asked suspiciously.

"Alex and I shared various adventures, various business ventures. Did I know him well? How well does one really know anyone?"

"If you were really his friend," I said coldly, "you would have known I wasn't his girlfriend. I just met him a few days ago, here on Maui."

Bill paused a moment, as if searching for words. "My dear, I hate to speak ill of the dead, but Alex.... How should I put this delicately? Alex 'got around.' So I was not at all surprised to learn that his current companion was a woman as attractive and charming as yourself."

"Oh," I said, slightly embarrassed. "I didn't mean to sound churlish. It's just that . . .."

"I quite understand. This has undoubtedly been difficult for you, no matter how brief—or superficial—your friendship was with Alex."

I looked at him curiously.

"I hope we can get to know each other better," he said.

I started to nibble on a cold barbecued rib, then dropped the unappetizing item back on the plate. "Just what are you getting at, Mr. Miller?"

"Call me Bill. By the way, I didn't catch your name . . .. "

"Noa. Noa Webster."

He smiled. "Any relation to Gauguin's mistress, Noa Noa? I mean the name, of course."

"Of course. Most people don't make the connection."

"I'm interested in the arts," he replied off-handedly, then turned and signaled to the waitress. When she came over, he ordered a Mai Tai and, before I could object, a refill for me.

Glancing at the plate of nearly untouched appetizers, he said, "Perhaps we could discuss this over dinner?"

"Why?"

"As two friends of Alex, I still think we might have a mutual interest."

"Alex, you mean?" I asked. "Or something else?"

"What else could we have in common? Aside from getting to know each other better, of course . . .."

Just then the band returned. With a white-toothed grin, the leader gestured to Aloha. "We have a special treat for all the *wahines*—that's ladies, folks—in our audience. Aloha has agreed to give a hula lesson to all of you! So come on up, lovely ladies, and try your hand—or should I say your hips—at it!"

Nobody moved.

"Now ladies, don't be bashful. You wouldn't want to disappoint your partners, would you?" he urged.

A low murmur in the audience indicated efforts were underway to encourage spouses/companions. With a giggle, the female half of the honeymoon couple stood up and came forward; the older woman in fluttering silks joined the ranks, as did the short-haired woman in the oversized T-shirt and the two sunburned girls. The band began to play "The Hukilau Song," and Aloha started to show the awkward *wahines* how to rhythmically swing their hips one way, their knees the other, while at the same time using their hands, arms, and heads to tell the story of a communal fishing feast. Next they imitated a fish swimming through the ocean and sang, with lots of giggles, the refrain to a song about the humuhumunukunukuapua'a, a fish whose redundant name is longer than it is.

I hate amateur talent shows.

Bill patiently repeated his offer of dinner.

"All right," I agreed, wondering if I could learn anything from him that would help me understand what was going on here.

"Good. How about Aloha?"

That's where Alex and I had had dinner the night before.

Taking my silence as agreement, he said, "Fine. I'll make reservations." He stood up. "I'll meet you in the lobby in half an hour. That'll give you time to change. I'm looking forward to this immense-

ly. Whatever Alex's faults, you could never fault his taste in women."
With an appreciative smile, he turned and left.

The man was smooth. Mild mannered, unobtrusive, but definitely
smooth. And definitely not to be trusted. I realized that he had managed to reveal almost nothing about himself or his real interest in
my connection with Alex. At the same time, he had made it appear
that he was sympathetic and, maybe, just a tiny bit interested in me.
Fortunately, I knew better. Foolishly, I thought I could outwit him at
his own game.

Six

When I reached my room, I noticed the door was slightly ajar. Cautiously pushing it open with my foot, I peered inside. The sun was just beginning its slow descent into the ocean, and it lit the shambles of my room with a gentle, pastel glow.

"Damn!" I muttered, then waited for a moment at the doorway, listening intently for the sound of breathing, the rustle of cloth, the shuffle of feet. When I was convinced that no one was there—after all, he/she/they had probably left the door open when they fled—I entered the room cautiously. Picking my way through the debris, I reached the phone and called the main desk. Then I called the police.

Larry answered the phone, not Nestor, and he sounded suitably concerned. No, they had not searched my room a second time. No, he had no idea who had. Don't touch a thing, he ordered. I've got to change for dinner, I declared. Wait right there, he demanded. Grudgingly, I agreed.

Don't get me wrong—I wasn't calm, I was upset. This wasn't the first time my room had been searched—once here and once in Spain. But believe me, you never get used to that stomach-wrenching sense of violation. This time, however, I felt angry, not anxious. I hadn't asked to be involved. In fact, I'd done everything I could not to be involved. But it had gotten me nowhere.

It was becoming clearer and clearer that the only choice I had was whether I would be involved in this situation passively, as a victim; or actively, as a sleuth, a hunter, a solver of puzzles, a finder of solutions. After my experience in Spain, I knew the latter was preferable. The more I thought about it, the more determined I was to solve the murder and the mystery of the missing *tikis*. Since the police were no help, I'd have to do it myself—and nobody, but nobody, had better stand in my way! Brave words, I knew, but saying them to myself made me feel better. Just like whistling in the dark.

This latest move simply confirmed what I already suspected: somebody other than Alex, me, and the *kahuna* knew about the *tiki*. For a moment, I wondered if the *kahuna* could have done it, but I quickly dismissed that idea. He'd had the *tiki* in his hands and he'd returned it to me. So who could it have been?

Impatiently, I waited on the walkway outside my room. Ten minutes later Larry and Nestor arrived and surveyed the damage. While we watched, the hotel staff silently straightened the overturned table and chairs, put the drawers back in the dresser, and generally reconstructed the room. Their silence was more unsettling than idle chatter. For a fleeting moment, I wondered if the hotel management would ask me to find a room somewhere else—like on a different island.

With Larry's gentle prodding, I provided a brief description of where I had been and when.

"By the way," he asked casually, "who are you having dinner with?"

"Bill. Bill Miller."

Nestor had been unusually subdued, but at this point he piped up, "Another 'friend' you just met?"

"I don't think that's any of your business," I replied coldly.

"Yeah? I'll be the judge of that."

Angrily, I turned to Larry, who just shrugged. "If you must know," I replied, "Bill Miller is a guest at the hotel. I met him downstairs in the patio."

"Bill Miller . . .. Name sounds familiar," Nestor muttered.

I ignored him and checked over my belongings. It didn't take long. I hadn't brought much—a small suitcase full of clothes, a briefcase full of papers. Nothing was missing.

"Any idea what they were after?" Larry asked.

Shaking my head, I replied, "No idea."

Eyes narrowed, Nestor probed, "How about the *tiki*? You sure they weren't after that?"

"How should I know!"

"Whatever it was, I guess they didn't find it," Larry replied.

"Guess not," I echoed.

"Well," Larry said, with false reassurance, "Whoever they are, we'll get 'em."

"Right. Hopefully before they get me."

"Why would they be after you?"

"No idea," I said, trying not to look at my bag.

Nestor snorted. "Don't forget, we're still checking out your connection with Alex."

"Remember," Larry said, "call me if anything unusual happens. Call me any time. You have my number."

I nodded. "Don't worry, I will."

The police left. The hotel staff left. And suddenly I felt all alone and very vulnerable.

The phone rang. It was Bill, inquiring about the delay. I told him I'd be right down.

Quickly, I threw on my special-occasion black silk dress, fastened my antique Navajo concho belt loosely around my waist, brushed my hair, put on some pink lipstick, and changed into high-heeled sandals. Then I dumped out the contents of my bag and selected a few items to put into the fake Channel eelskin purse I had bought the day before. The *tiki* made a slight bulge, but there was nothing I could do about it. I wasn't going to leave it behind.

Bill was waiting in the lobby, looking a trifle annoyed.

"Sorry I'm late," I said, "but I was unavoidably detained."

He lifted one eyebrow. "Nothing serious, I hope."

"Yes and no. My room had been ransacked, and I had to wait for the police to come."

"Anything taken?"

"Not that I could find."

Sympathetically, he said, "You seem to be having more than your share of trouble! If I can help, let me know." He paused for a moment. "I hope you don't mind, but I thought we would walk along the beach to the restaurant."

"No problem. I like to walk."

He looked at my high heels.

"I'll just take them off."

He looked at me and smiled in approval, or so I thought at the time.

We strolled out of the lobby, through the tropical garden, and past the patio. The band was still playing, but the audience had thinned out. Only the single woman, the older woman and her friend, and the lovers remained.

We ambled slowly towards the Royal Princess in a companionable silence, as if we were old friends. Sometimes it happens that way—two strangers meet and immediately begin to play subtle games. Maybe we were both carefully rehearsing what to say and what not to say during the evening ahead. Whatever the reason, I appreciated the silence. The sand felt warm and giving beneath my bare feet, and I enjoyed the balmy night air and the delicate slurping of the water as it sucked up the grains of sand. The sun had not yet set, but the first evening star—I suppose it was Venus, so it was actually a planet—was faintly visible. Silently I made a wish.

I must have sighed.

Bill said softly, "A penny for your thoughts."

I laughed a bit self-consciously. "I was just thinking about how gorgeous it is here. But relaxing—and pleasant—it hasn't been."

He smiled sympathetically. "Your first visit to the islands?"

"Mmhmm. And yours?"

"No, I've been here a few times before, for business and pleasure."

"With Alex?"

"Sometimes, sometimes not. It is beautiful here, isn't it. Have you had a chance to see much of Maui?"

"Not much. Yesterday—I can't believe it was only yesterday—I did some sightseeing with Alex."

"Where did you go?"

"We took an Aloha Tour excursion on the Road to Hana." I paused for a moment. "I suppose that's odd, come to think of it. After all, Alex was from Hawaii. So why would he want to go on a tourist excursion? Unless, of course, he wanted to look like a tourist."

Bill replied slowly, "Just what are you getting at?"

"Maybe it was for protective coloration," I mused aloud. Suddenly I realized that I might be giving something away. "I mean, after all, Alex gave me a false name. Maybe he was hiding out."

"From whom?"

"Beats me. I thought you might have an idea. After all, you were his friend and—didn't you say—sometime business partner?"

With a frown, he shrugged his shoulders.

Soon we reached the elaborately landscaped grounds of the Royal Princess. Unlike the Maui Surfside, there were no dunes between the hotel and the beach, but there was an extensive Japanese-style garden, a small golf course, and a large clearing for the *luau* celebration. We followed the path to the hotel, then climbed the wide, tile-paved staircase to the lobby.

Interspersed between ten-foot-tall Christmas trees decorated with white origami doves were half a dozen gingerbread houses. These were not your regular cookie-cutter confections, however; each elaborate construction was about six feet tall and mounted on a pedestal surrounded by fence—white picket, rustic log, etc.—in keeping with the style of the house. I expected mechanized elves to appear at the windows, but, fortunately, the designers had exercised some restraint.

We took the elevator to the Aloha restaurant on the second floor. It was elegant—dark teakwood walls, white linen tablecloths, enormous damask napkins, glittering crystal goblets, heavy engraved silverware. Museum-quality Asian art hung on the walls and adorned the corners, and a multitude of waiters, filling and refilling, bringing and removing, glided soundlessly through the dining room.

As was apparently typical of Hawaiian resort hotels, the exterior walls were only waist-high, so the heavy scent of tropical blossoms floated up from the garden, intermingling with the aroma of herbs and spices and sizzling meats. The twittering of birds and the lapping of the waves melded with the low murmur of voices. Ah, paradise.

At Bill's suggestion—he'd eaten there a number of times, he explained—we shared a selection of hors d'oeuvres, including a pâté of venison served with mango and papaya chutney, and batter-fried chunks of lobster served with bittersweet *hoisin* and honey mustard dipping sauces. Also at his suggestion, I ordered island snapper, wrapped in filo pastry and stuffed with shrimp and wild Haiku mushrooms; Bill ordered rare-roasted Ulupalakua lamb with mustard rosemary seasoning. When the waiter placed our selections in front of us, I simply inhaled the exquisite aromas for a moment. Bill laughed at the expression on my face, then offered me a bite of his crusty, succulent lamb.

I don't remember the names of the wines—Maui something—local wines, to go with local produce. A bit sweet, but very good. After we finished the main course we had the house salad of arugula, Belgian endive, sweet Maui onions, and chunks of apples and walnuts, sprinkled with fresh-grated Parmesan.

During dinner I learned nothing about Bill's connection with Alex, but I did learn that Bill came from California. Despite my intentions to "pump" Bill, we spent dinner talking about very little except food—memorable meals we had had, intriguing dinner companions, unusual dishes. I don't think it was a planned evasion on either of our parts. I've noticed before that a really good meal often stimulates recollection of other fine meals, of vivid memories that, retold, intensify the current gastronomic pleasure.

While we contemplated the selection of desserts that was wheeled up to us on a gleaming chrome cart, we drank steaming Kona coffee, topped with a dollop of whipped cream. Bill chose a relatively mundane macadamia-nut pie, but I selected a ginger-tinged meringue, lightly brushed with chocolate, its empty center filled with a fresh raspberry sauce. The crunchy meringue, the hardened chocolate, the soft, almost syrupy raspberries engaged all senses. I admit it—if I could afford it, I would be a Sybarite.

Seeing my expression of unabashed pleasure, Bill leaned back in his chair and laughed.

Slightly embarrassed, I laughed as well.

"I can see why Alex was so taken with you," Bill said.

Startled, I replied, "For a moment, I had forgotten what brought us together."

Bill made a little A-frame tent with his hands and frowned. "So had I. But I suppose it's time to get down to business."

Expectantly, I looked at him over the delicate, gilded rim of my porcelain coffee cup.

"I said earlier that I thought we might have a common interest."

"So you did," I murmured.

"I realize from what you've told me that you really didn't know Alex very well."

"I realize that now, too," I agreed.

"You know even less about me. So let me begin by giving you a bit of background. He and I go way back. We met—it doesn't matter where—and found we shared several interests. Sailing, for one. Travel, for another." He glanced at me. "Art, for yet another."

"Art?"

"Art. But not just any art. Special art. Art with a soul, with a history."

Cautiously, I nodded my head.

"On occasion, Alex learned about special . . . shall we say . . . opportunities? Together, we took advantage of several, to our mutual benefit."

"Yes?" I said, with what I hoped was the right mixture of curiosity, caution, and encouragement.

"Alex had his sources, and I had my contacts. Together, we did quite well on several occasions."

"Yes?"

He hesitated a moment, then signaled to the hovering waiter and whispered something. The waiter disappeared.

"You have to understand, my dear, how foolish some of the restrictions are that govern the buying and selling of antiquities. What is old in one country is modern in another. A crude, worm-eaten carving, for example, may have little intrinsic value, but to the right collector, it can be worth a great deal. Alex was such a collector."

"I see," I said noncommittally.

The waiter returned with two large brandy snifters, which he placed in front of us. Bill nodded, and he retreated once again.

Picking up the snifter, Bill swirled the amber liquid around. Then he looked directly at me and said, "Alex was engaged in a project which he had seen fit to inform me about. I came immediately to assist him. But before I had the chance to meet with him, he was brutally murdered."

"Oh," I said, picking up my brandy snifter and swirling the heavy amber liquid, watching the "legs" form and flow down the smooth glass sides. "I see."

"I thought you would."

I asked carefully, "When did you say you arrived?"

"Last night."

"From where did you say?"

"I didn't. From California."

For a moment, we both sipped the fragrant, floral-scented brandy. Then I asked, "When were you supposed to meet Alex?"

"This morning, around 10 o'clock."

"Why not last night?"

"I don't understand what you're getting at," he said slowly.

As innocently as possible, I replied, "I just wondered why, if this meeting were so important, you didn't see him the moment you got in?"

"He didn't know exactly when I was arriving. He called me Thursday, and I told him I would get here as quickly as possible. However, he wasn't in his room when I arrived. Apparently, he was out with you. That was typical of him, I'm afraid. He let his attention wander from the task at hand. So I left a message for him, and he left me a message that he would meet me at 10 this morning."

"Oh."

"So you see," Bill said carefully, "It would definitely be to your advantage to tell me anything that might be relevant."

"I'm afraid I don't understand," I said, with as ingenuous an expression as I could muster.

A bit impatiently, he replied, "Perhaps Alex mentioned something directly to you that might help me locate the missing objects."

"Oh," I said brightly, "Now I understand. Alex had something to sell you—some art object—and you don't know what's happened to it. Is that it?"

"That's it precisely. I could make it worth your while, my dear."

"But wouldn't this be a matter for the police?" I asked.

"I'm sure they won't be interested."

"You're sure?"

"Of course I'm sure!" A dangerous edge had crept into his voice. "Besides, if you were going to go to the police, you would have gone already."

"What do you mean?" I replied, my voice suddenly hoarse.

"I saw you and Alex this morning, playing with a *tiki*. One of four missing *tikis*. That's what I mean."

"You saw us?"

"So you see," he said, with a no-longer-so-enchanting smile, "I believe we do share a common interest. You have something I want. And I usually get what I want."

Now I knew what it meant when a writer writes, "the silence was deafening." Frantically, I tried to think of the most innocuous reply, the least damaging, the most self-protective. My mind went blank. I glanced up and saw he was staring at me, and his bland, unremarkable appearance no longer looked quite so innocent. It was all very carefully cultivated in order to avoid being memorable.

His manicured hands drummed on the table, and I wondered whether they could have lifted a large rock and smashed Alex on the back of the head, then dragged him into the Jacuzzi. After all, he'd been at the hotel this morning. He'd seen Alex. He'd seen the *tiki*. And he'd seen me. Maybe Alex had tried to double-cross him, or change the price. Maybe that was the appointment Alex had run off to meet— but no, that was too early. Unless Bill was lying about the time of his appointment.

My head felt like it would split apart, but not from the brandy.

I took a deep breath. "Look, Bill, I really don't know anything more than I already told you and the police."

Startled, he replied, "The police?"

"Yes, the police. I told them about the *tiki*. But I didn't have it. I had had it—Alex had slipped it into my bag—but it disappeared. At the time I didn't think it was important."

Eyes narrowed, Bill stared at me.

"It's true," I said defensively. "An old Hawaiian priest stopped by to visit me, and he took the *tiki*."

"A *kahuna*?"

I nodded. "That's what he said. Believe me, I couldn't make this up if I tried. I'm an anthropologist, not a novelist. He saw the *tiki* on my dresser and told me about it. And then he disappeared, along with the *tiki*. I told the police, but they didn't believe me." I looked him in the eyes. "Obviously, neither do you."

Bill drummed his fingers on the table some more, then leaned towards me. "Your story is unlikely enough to be true." He seemed lost in thought for a moment, then continued, "I think I believe you. For the time being, at least. But that doesn't really change anything. My offer still stands. Alex is dead, and you are the only one who can help me find the *tikis*. Believe me, I'll make it worth your while."

I looked away. Everybody wanted my help, except the police.

"Think about it. And remember, my dear, I simply can't abide being double-crossed." He gestured towards the waiter, and handed him a platinum credit card. After signing the receipt, he stood up. Slowly, I stood up also.

With a grim smile, Bill said, "My dear, you are mixed up in a very dangerous game, whether you want to be or not. You'll need all the protection you can find. Remember what happened to Alex."

Trying to look calm, I asked, "Is that a threat?"

"Consider it a cautionary reminder."

In wary silence, we walked back up the beach to the hotel, and Bill saw me to my room.

At the door, I turned to him and said, "The *kahuna* seemed to think the *tikis* belonged to him—or, rather, to the Hawaiian people."

"And what will he—or they—do with them?" Bill said with obvious disgust. "In no time, they'll be destroyed, or stolen, and that will be the end of them. These glorious objects will be lost forever."

"While you'll sell them to the highest bidder, correct?"

"They will be well preserved and properly appreciated, believe me."

"Believe me, I do."

"Remember what I've said—you've gotten yourself in the middle of a very dangerous game. Let me correct myself. It's not a game. It's dead serious." His voice softened. "But we can discuss this again tomorrow. Breakfast, shall we say? At Trifles? At 8?"

With a shaky smile, I said, "Better make it 9. I plan to sleep late."

"Sleep well, my dear." With a slight bow, he turned and walked down the corridor.

I watched till he was out of sight. Then I unlocked the door and went inside. This time, at least, no one had been there before me.

Seven

Contrary my own expectations, I slept soundly. I awakened suddenly, at sunrise, just in time to watch the full moon sink into the ink-green ocean. To the northwest I could see the West Maui Mountains, veiled in a pale, pink-tinged mist that was just starting to burn off.

Eager to enjoy the early morning air, I quickly got dressed for a walk on the beach. But then, on second thought, I regretfully decided to forego my solitary walk. No point in making it easy for the killer. Or killers.

The killer's anonymity was increasingly disturbing. Who had murdered Alex? Could it have been the *kahuna*? He said he had arrived after the murder, but had he? Could it have been his granddaughter Melemele? Or the mysterious "Mrs. Bainbridge," if such a person actually existed? Could it have been Bill, or possibly, his partners? After all, I only had his word for it that he was working alone. Maybe, for safety's sake, I should assume there was more than one person involved in the murder. Or maybe it had been just an accident, and Alex had somehow smashed his head in the Jacuzzi. I shook my head sadly as brutal reality intruded. I knew better than that. Alex's death was no accident.

Glancing around the hotel room, I wondered who had trashed it. Some or all of the above? Could it have been the police, despite their denial? After all, my room had been searched twice, once with a search warrant and once after I told the police about the *tiki*. Nestor was so offensive, I was beginning to wonder if he was deviously calculating instead of obnoxiously stupid. And what about Larry? Unlikely as it seemed, could he be a secret follower of the *kahuna*?

Was the same person (or people) responsible for Alex's murder and for searching my room, or were these separate events? After all, if someone wanted the *tikis*, why would they have killed Alex before they got them? One last question: where were the other *tikis*, and how could I possibly find them? And was I really going to try?

After a few fruitless minutes, I quit trying to figure anything out. My mind doesn't really start to function until I've had a cup—or two or three cups—of coffee. Since I didn't want to wait until breakfast with Bill Miller, and I didn't feel like going to the other hotel restaurant, I called room service.

A lilting voice answered, "*Aloha kakahiaka.* Good morning. How can we help you?"

"I'd like coffee."

"What kind?"

"Strong," I muttered, my morning voice rusty from lack of use.

"We have a number of flavors. We have raspberry truffle, Kona, Maui sunrise, chocolate coconut, chocolate-macadamia-nut—"

"I'll take the last one."

"Mahalo. Thank you," she chirped.

The bellboy arrived almost immediately, pushing a bamboo cart that contained a complete coffee service, including little bowls filled with chocolate curlicues, cinnamon sticks, and whipped cream, and a Maui Surfside-emblazoned mug. With a graceful flourish, he placed the contents on the table on the *lanai.*

"The mug is a gift from the management," he explained.

Pleasantly surprised, I didn't even blanche at the bill.

"*Mahalo nui loa,*" he said with an appreciative grin as he pocketed the outrageously generous tip. I might be a slow learner, but I was learning.

Drinking the fragrant coffee was like imbibing liquid dessert but without the calories. Contented, I watched the motorboats moving out to sea. Some, I knew, were heading to Molokini, the nearby, crescent-shaped remains of an ancient volcano. Snorkeling was supposed to be quite good in the sheltered cove. Bouncing rubber Zodiacs skipped like pebbles over the ocean, hugging the coast before heading out across the open expanse of water. Only for the brave, I thought, or for those needing inexpensive transportation. In the distance a parasail began uncoiling from its boat and soon the colorful glider floated like an enormous tropical bird high above the sea, its rider dangling from a swinging seat suspended just below its wings.

I wanted to go snorkeling, I wanted to see whales, I wanted to have fun. I did not want to go parasailing. I'm afraid of heights. More than anything, I wanted to have a vacation in paradise. Was that asking so much? Ruefully, I nodded my head. I had a gut feeling that until I found the *tikis,* or Alex's murderer, I would not be having much fun on Maui. Already, I was not having much fun.

An insistent knocking got my attention. Room service again?

Framed in the doorway were two men I had seen at the hula performance the night before. The short, comb-over one was pinch-nosed and squint-eyed. He was wearing a wrinkled brown Hawaiian shirt patterned with green and yellow pineapples, beige shorts, white socks, and black lace-up shoes. His companion, the red-headed man, was equally unappealing. His face was sunburned, his nose bulbous, and he had a large pot belly that strained the buttons on his stained white shirt. He was wearing a baggy jacket, which seemed odd. Nobody wears a jacket in Hawaii, not even to a fancy restaurant. He kept hitching up his equally baggy khaki pants. He looked like he was wearing someone else's clothes.

Neither of the two exactly inspired confidence.

"Yes?" I asked, trying to sound neutral instead of nervous.

"Ahem," said the medium-height one, clearing his throat. "We're here about the death of one Alexander Bainbridge." His voice was raw at the edges, and he reeked of cigarettes. I hate the smell of cigarettes. I used to smoke, and there is nothing as intolerant as a reformed smoker—except a reformed something else.

"Yeah," added the short one, in a surprisingly deep voice. "We're insurance investigators. I'm Joe, and this is my partner, Sam." He took out a worn-looking wallet and flashed a laminated card at me, then slipped it back in his rear pocket.

"I don't think there's anything I can tell you," I said. "Why don't you talk to the police?"

"We done that already. We want to talk to you."

"Who did you say you were?" I asked, suspiciously.

"Like I told you, insurance investigators. We know you found the body, and we want to talk to you. We're looking for some property of his that belongs to a client of ours," Joe said.

"Property?"

"What he means is, we're investigating the situation for our company," Sam interrupted. "Was there anything unusual about Mr. Bainbridge before he died? Did he act strange, or say anything funny?"

"I don't think . . . ."

"Mind if we come in?" Joe said and started to push into the room.

Angrily, I stood my ground. "Yes, I do mind. One more step and I'll call the police!"

"Now, lady, you wouldn't want to do that," Sam said soothingly. "We only want to ask you some questions. Don't get all steamed."

"Out!" I demanded.

They glanced at each other and advanced towards me. Unwillingly, I started to back up.

The room was getting a little crowded.

Joe and Sam moved towards me and I raced towards the phone.

I picked it up and started to dial.

Joe lunged towards me and grabbed my arm, forcing me to drop the phone.

"Let go of me!"

"All we wanna do is ask you some questions, lady. Don't make it difficult," Joe growled.

"I'll scream—"

"Don't do anything stupid," Sam said in a bored, irritated voice.

I took a deep breath and got ready to scream.

Just then David, the *kahuna*, appeared in the doorway.

"Can I help?" he asked as he walked in.

Sam started to reach into his jacket, but in one incredibly swift movement David leaped into the air and kicked him in the side. Before I could even gasp, Sam lay curled up on the floor in a fetal position, holding his side and groaning.

Solidly back on both feet, David was not even breathing heavily. Joe's hold on my arm had loosened, and I immediately jerked free and backed away toward David. Keeping as far away from David as possible, Joe helped Sam stand up and limp to the door.

With a foul look, Sam turned and spat, "I'll getcha for this. You wait and see!"

As soon as they were gone, I exclaimed, "You sure got here at the right time!"

David smiled tranquilly. "I said I would be back."

"What was that, anyway—kung fu? Tai chi?"

"We *kahunas* know many things."

"I guess they teach you more than just how to pray."

"There are many ways to worship." He picked his hat up from the floor. "By the way, who were they?"

"They said they were insurance investigators, but if so, they must work for a really sleazy outfit."

"What did they want?"

"What you and everybody else wants. Information about the *tikis*."

"Me and everybody else?"

"You, and the police, and Bill, and—"

"Who is Bill?"

"Bill Miller. An art dealer. Actually, I think he's what's called a 'fence.'"

"How does he know about the *tikis*?"

"He says he was a friend and business partner of Alex's, and I believe him."

David frowned. "We must find the *tikis* as soon as possible. Your life may be in danger."

"I'm beginning to realize that. But I'm not sure my life won't be in danger even after I find the *tikis*. If I do."

"Why do you say that?"

"Because whoever wants the *tikis* must know something about the murder or may even be the murderer."

David shook his head. "That is not necessarily true. After all, I want the *tikis*. Do you think I am the murderer?"

Protesting a bit too vigorously, I replied, "Of course not!"

"So you see, the two things may be completely separate. We must worry about one thing at a time. First the *tikis*."

"Right. Come to think of it, I should be pretty safe until I find the *tikis*. They won't kill me if I'm the only one who knows—or whom they think knows—where the *tikis* are," I said, feeling slightly reassured. "But how do we find them?"

"You have not remembered anything?"

"I don't know what to remember," I pointed out.

"That is true." David paused a moment, thoughtfully. "I came here this morning with an idea. Perhaps if you and me and my granddaughter—"

"Your granddaughter? You found her?"

"She is staying with a friend. She and Alex were going to be engaged, so she is very unhappy. But she will be all right."

"Of course," I murmured. "You were saying?"

"We could all spend some time together. Melemele knew Alex very well, so perhaps something will remind you . . .."

"Just what did you have in mind?"

"My granddaughter wishes to visit a *heiau*, an ancient temple, and make an offering for Alex to our gods. I am inviting you to come along."

"I would like that very much," I replied sincerely, feeling the need to observe some kind of mourning ritual for Alex. Besides, my anthropological curiosity was aroused. "When do we leave?"

"As soon as possible. My *mo'opuna*—my granddaughter must work later today, so we must go now."

I looked at my watch. 8:30. "I'm supposed to have breakfast with Bill but I'll tell him I can't make it."

"Good."

After debating whether to call Bill or leave a message, I decided on the latter. That way I could avoid a direct confrontation and a lengthy explanation. I picked up my bag—the one with the *tiki* inside—and David and I headed down the walkway. When we reached the stairs, David hesitated.

"You have a car?"

"Yes."

"Good. Then you can drive."

"No problem."

"It is parked in the hotel garage?"

"Yes."

"I will meet you there." He started to walk away.

"Wait—why are you leaving?" I called after him.

"I do not think it wise to be seen together. It is not safe for you."

Puzzled, I watched him disappear around a corner. Then I hurried down the path to the lobby, glancing frequently over my shoulder. I left a cryptic message at the reception desk for Bill. "Sorry, change of plans. Back later."

When I reached the garage, David stepped out from behind a column. I jumped back in fright.

"You startled me!"

"You must learn to be more watchful. It is very dangerous for you now."

He was probably right, I realized. I would have to be much more careful.

Following his directions, I drove towards town, then took a narrow side road that led "upcountry" towards the dormant volcano, Haleakala. At last we came to a small, shabby house, its paint peeling. Several rusting cars rested, immobile, in the front yard, shaded by shaggy palm trees. I pulled into the gravel driveway and waited by the side of the car while David went around to the back.

After a few minutes he returned. Walking morosely beside him was the beautiful hula dancer, Aloha.

Eight

"She's your granddaughter?" I exclaimed.

"Of course. Why are you surprised?" David asked.

"But her name's Aloha!"

"That's my stage name," she replied in the flat, moody voice I had heard the night before.

"I saw you dance at the Maui Surfside last night. You were wonderful!" I gushed.

Her large, chocolate-brown eyes stared dully at me. I had the feeling no one was home.

"Melemele is a fine dancer. She has been trained since childhood with the best *hula halau* on the island to dance the sacred *hulas*," David explained proudly. "Unfortunately, she must earn a living doing popular dances for *haole*."

"It's okay, Grandfather. I like to dance."

"And you're so good at it," I said. "But it can't be much fun to teach *wahines* the "Little Grass Shack.""

"It's just part of the job," she replied, indifferently, sliding into the back seat. She carefully placed a large pink nylon beach bag on the seat beside her. David got into the passenger side in front.

"Where to?" I asked.

"Go back past the hotel and towards Makena," David directed.

I nodded. "Just tell me where and when to turn."

As my eyes flicked back and forth between the road in front and the rear-view mirror, I caught glimpses of a tense-faced Melemele staring sullenly out the window. Even wearing a cheap, green terry jumpsuit, she was gorgeous. How could someone that beautiful be so ill humored? Maybe I was being too harsh, I chided myself. After all, Alex's death must have been very upsetting. Maybe she was normally a happy-go-lucky child of paradise.

Trying to make conversation, I said sympathetically, "I'm sure it must have been quite a shock to learn about Alex's death."

"You said it. A real shock," she answered, voice flat.

"Your grandfather says you were going to be married."

"That's right. Thursday Alex told me we were going to get engaged to be engaged," she said, chewing on a ragged fingernail.

"Isn't that a bit odd?" I asked.

"What?"

"Well," I said hesitantly, "I always thought people got engaged to get married. Is this something new—to get engaged to get engaged?"

"Maybe it was kind of a joke, you know, to say it that way?" she replied. "Alex was always joking. Anyway, we were going to get engaged. I was so excited I called Grandfather first thing the next day to tell him."

"I was glad she was settling down. She's had so many boy-friends...." David said.

"Grandfather!" Melemele replied, outraged. At last she had some animation in her voice.

"It's true, Melemele. I've lost track, there've been so many. Most of them I never even met, they came and went so fast. I just want you to be happy, that's all, and I don't think that's the way."

"You didn't tell me you knew Alex," I said to David, puzzled by this omission.

The *kahuna* didn't say anything.

Melemele replied, "I introduced them. Alex was interested in old Hawaii, and my grandfather is a *kahuna*."

"Yes, I know."

"I thought Alex would like to meet him. They got along okay."

David nodded. "He seemed to be a good man, even though he had so much money. His wealth made it easy for him to get what he wanted. Maybe too easy. But he seemed to have the right attitude."

"Right attitude?" I asked.

"His ancestors—the *haole*, the foreigners who invaded our country—destroyed our way of life, and he wanted to make up for that. Nothing could make up for that, but he seemed sincere. He said he wanted to learn about the old ways."

"Oh," I said, intrigued by this previously unknown side of Alex. "But how did he get involved with the theft of the *tikis*?"

"I told him the *tiki* figures belonged to the ancient people of Hawaii," David explained. "He knew how I felt about that. He knew how important they were to our people."

"But that doesn't explain how he got the *tiki*."

"No." David looked out the window.

We sped past the Maui Surfside, then past the Royal Princess. Following directions, I turned off the highway to take a narrow rutted road that followed closer to the coast. We drove by a Hawaii Visitors Bureau Warrior, a wooden marker in the shape of a dark-skinned Hawaiian in a yellow and red robe and crested helmet. The warrior pointed towards a nearby building surrounded by tropical trees—fan-shaped traveler palms, fragrant plumeria, bushy jacaranda. According to the sign, the gray stucco, shingle-roofed building was the Keawala'i Congregational church, built in 1832. An overgrown cemetery was located behind the church, and a narrow path beside the graveyard led to the beach just beyond.

The moody silence of my companions wasn't getting us anywhere, and it was somewhat puzzling. After all, according to David, the idea of the joint excursion was to trigger some memory about where the *tikis* were hidden, and we couldn't do that without talking.

Glancing in the rearview mirror, I asked, "Melemele, did you know a friend of Alex's named Al?"

She shook her head.

"You sure? Alex said he was an old friend."

"I didn't know any of his friends," she said, then returned to staring out the window.

I tried again. "Did you know Alex very long?"

This time there was no response. After a moment, David replied, "She met him a few months ago." Then he, too, lapsed back into silence.

I gave up.

Soon we passed a sign for Makena beach, which, according to Alex, was famous for excellent snorkeling and nude bathing. In the late 1960s the area was home to a large hippie community. Insufficient waste disposal, contaminated water, and a variety of diseases and drugs made the area less than idyllic, and in 1972 the police evicted the settlers. The vestiges of the "back to nature" movement remained, however, in the form of nude bathing at the nearby Little Beach. At least, that's what Alex had told me. He'd promised to take me there, but he hadn't had the chance.

Dense groves of twisted trees extended along the coast. They reminded me of my childhood in the Southwest. "Aren't those mesquite?" I asked.

"I don't know. We call them *kiawe*. The *haole* brought them. The wood is useful, but the trees have sharp thorns," David said.

When we swung back up to the main road, I was surprised to see how different this part of the island looked. On the ocean side of the road, major construction was underway to build more hotels and condos, construction that was destroying the very things that people came to Maui to see—tropical beauty and uncrowded beaches. Soon the island would be swarming with more tourists that it could hold, and they would see not natural beauty but some artificial construct, complete with swimming pools and golf courses and fake waterfalls.

Once we got past the construction, the countryside looked relatively undisturbed, but it didn't look tropical. Thickets of gray-green prickly pear cactuses, some fifteen feet tall, dotted the landscape, taking over the scruffy-looking range where cattle roamed.

"Where did the cactus come from? Surely it isn't native," I asked.

With a shrug, David replied, "We think the *panioli*—the Spanish-Portuguese cowboys—brought it with them, to remind them of home. Or maybe the seeds came in cattle feed. The thorns are painful, so we call the cactus *panini*—'very unfriendly,' in Hawaiian. It also was brought by the *haole*."

"Didn't the white man bring anything good?" I asked.

"Reading, perhaps. And writing. Democracy instead of monarchy. But that only meant that the white men could legally rule Hawaii, and all Hawaiians were powerless. Has the evil been balanced by the good? I don't think so."

"But you—I mean, the Hawaiian people—couldn't have remained isolated forever."

"That is true. But the land, and our way of living, did not have to be destroyed. You are an anthropologist. You should understand."

He was right. I should.

"That's why we have a strong Hawaiian sovereignty movement. We seek self-determination and self-governance for Native Hawaiians. Among other things, we want redress from your country for over-throwing Queen Lili'uokalani in 1893 and for your military occupation beginning in 1898."

"That was a long time ago, wasn't it?"

"That's no excuse."

Melemele roused herself for a moment. "Grandfather feels real strongly about this. He's been part of the movement since the 1970s when it first started."

"Long before you were born, Granddaughter. Long before you were born," David said, nodding. "It's been a long fight."

The road narrowed even more. On the left, partly hidden by low-lying clouds, was the lush, verdant slope of Haleakala. On the coast-side of the road were small tropical-style houses on stilts, nearly hidden in dense foliage. We passed more groves of gnarled *kiawe* trees, a crumbled stone wall, and a wooden sign announcing that we were entering the Ahihi-Kinau Natural Reserve. The road dipped and twist-ed as it skirted the edge of the shore; the pounding surf was steadily wearing away the rough volcanic rock and had even begun nibbling at the side of the pavement.

"I hope I don't meet anyone," I observed, "The road's not wide enough for two, and there's nowhere to pull off."

"Few people come this way. And they come slowly," David replied.

Soon we came to a hand-lettered sign that said, "CAUTION: sim-ulated moon surface." It did not bode well.

Climbing up an incline we emerged onto a rusty black, blasted moonscape. Lava coughed up from Haleakala's side two centuries before had flowed down the slope and sizzled into the sea. Some of these cinders had fused together into grotesque lumps; others were loose, scattered at random over the top of the relatively newly formed peninsula.

Nothing grew on the jumbled surface. Nothing moved across it, not even birds.

What passed for a road was cut through the lava. It looked suitable for four-wheel drive vehicles only, not rental cars. I seemed to remember my rental agreement forbade taking the car on certain unpaved roads. I wondered whether this even counted as an unpaved road. I slowed down and looked questioningly at David.

He nodded. "Keep going."

With a sigh, I continued, carefully steering between the ruts. Only the pounding of the surf against the lava and the puttering of the car's motor broke the silence. Every so often the road widened a bit, probably so that less intrepid—or wiser—travelers could stop and turn around. We continued for several miles, past a sign, "La Pérouse Bay," named after the first non-Hawaiian, a Frenchman, to set foot on Maui. After we drove by an enormous estate, dramatically located at the edge of the bay, the road petered out. A faint foot trail stretched into the distance. We could drive no further.

Vaguely uneasy, I stopped the car and we got out.

Pointing at the path, David explained, "This is the remains of the Hoapili, the King's Trail. We will follow it to the temple."

David led the way. I brought up the rear.

To say the landscape was desolate would be an understatement. The narrow King's Trail led straight across the lava flow. Up close, I could see green splotches of weeds and gray lichens taking hold, beginning the long slow process of dissolution that would turn the lava into fertile soil. But it would take a while. Centuries. Meanwhile, we picked our way across the rough, cinder-strewn path. Stretching into the distance and down to the sea, the rusted-looking chunks of sharp-edged lava smothered the barren land.

I picked up a fist-sized piece of *a'a*. It looked like pumice, but it was heavy, much heavier than I expected. I wondered whether the molten minerals had condensed as they hardened. It was slightly warm, as if it had absorbed the light and heat of the sun and wouldn't give it back.

Every so often I saw what looked like a cairn of large clinkers. Eager to break the eerie silence, I asked David, "Are those stacks of lava natural or did someone pile them up that way?"

He trudged along ahead. After a moment, he said, "They are markers."

"What do they mark?"

"Offerings."

I looked more closely and could see little cubbyholes at the base of the stacks.

We continued on in silence. The landscape, as well as the reason for our journey, seemed to demand silence.

Our trail crossed a patchwork of old lava and new grass, areas where the flowing fingers of liquid rock had failed to cover the land completely. As we skirted the coast, I could see tiny patches of beaches, scattered pockets of black and white sand, coral rubble, and various-sized rocks. A lone native fisherman cast his line into the surf. Apparently he, too, had come on foot.

At last we came to a lava flow that jutted out further than the rest, then dropped abruptly into the sea. The foot-high, ruined walls of a large rectangular stone platform were still visible.

"We have reached our destination," David said.

Stating the not so obvious, I said, "This is a *heiau*?"

"Yes. Our people worshipped here and in others like this one but much larger, as large as a football field. In the old days, a wood frame covered with leaves and grass sheltered the altar, but that was destroyed long ago." He pointed to the remains of a large stone altar. "We made sacrifices here. Fish, dogs, chicken, decorated tapa cloth.

Sometimes we sacrificed humans on the altars. Especially we sacrificed those who violated *kapu*."

I shivered involuntarily. The *kahuna* had a disconcerting way of referring to the past and past wrongs as if he had been there and they had been done to him, not his ancestors. Racial memory? Or did he just have an overactive imagination? I wondered whether this was what Robert had meant when he said the *kahuna* had a "bee in his bonnet."

Suddenly I wondered if it had been a mistake to come to this isolated spot with David and Melemele. After all, what did I really know about either of them? I told myself I was being foolish. I hadn't done anything wrong. Besides, David had come to my rescue just a few hours before. He was on my side. Wasn't he?

He gestured wide with his hands. "Some *heiau* were sanctuaries, temples of refuge for the poor, the weak, the helpless. Others were places where oracles resided. Especially gifted *kahunas* could hear them speak. In the *heiau*, we could call to our gods. But now . . . now, this is all that is left."

Suddenly David had become positively loquacious.

Melemele put down the pink nylon bag and unzipped it, taking out a bundle of what looked like ferns, a delicately printed tapa cloth, and two calabashes lashed together. There was a hole in the end of the smaller one. She handed the calabash to David, who struck it several times with the palm of his hand. The sound was surprisingly deep and resonant.

He turned to me. "This is called an *ipu*. It is a traditional musical instrument. I will play it and chant the sacred *mele*. But first, let me tell you about my people."

He gestured for me to sit on the crumbled temple wall, and I sat. Melemele sat next to me.

Standing with his legs firmly planted on the stone platform, looking like an ancient Hawaiian demigod, the *kahuna* recited a mixture of myth/legend/history, learned by rote and flickering campfire light.

"More than one thousand five hundred years ago my people came to these islands, over the ocean they came from the Marquesas, thousands of miles to the south. They were brave people, my ancestors, traveling the huge, empty ocean, guided only by their knowledge of sky and stars, sea and currents, the flight of birds. In huge double-hulled canoes entire families came, as many as thirty people sailing together in a single canoe.

"Hundreds of years later other people came to the islands, too; some were sailors, lost at sea, some were invaders, seeking to conquer. They came and became part of our people. The Tahitians came and became part of us. The Polynesians came and became part of us. They brought sugarcane and banana, coconut and sweet potato, dogs and chickens, and pigs. But then the white man, the *haole*, came, and he did not become part of us. He brought disease and destruction and death.

"Before the white man came, we were a healthy, thriving people. We were ruled by mighty kings and mighty gods. We worshipped the forces of nature, and we carved their shapes out of the wood of the *ohi'a lehua* tree, a tree sacred to Pele, goddess of fire and volcanoes.

"Our people obeyed their kings and their priests. We had many rules, called *kapu*. These rules—what you call taboos—were our laws. They were sacred laws, and they were strict. They kept order in our lives.

"But then Captain Cook came and saw our riches and wanted them. We killed him. Our great king Kamehameha had already been born, but not even he could stop the white man, the *haole*, from coming.

"Thunder and a fiery comet announced Kamehameha's birth. His father tried to have him killed, but his mother hid him in the mountains. He grew up to be a brave leader and a fierce warrior. He was a big man, over six feet tall, and very strong. He became keeper of the war god, Kukailimoku, Ku of the Bloody Red Mouth, Ku the Destroyer.

"At last, with the help of the gods, and his brave followers, Kamehameha conquered the seven Hawaiian islands and united them under his rule. He was a just ruler and a wise one, and he used the white men to help him rule, but he did not let them rule him."

Melemele shifted impatiently on the rocks beside me. I bet she'd heard all this more than once before.

"But the *haole*, kept coming. They destroyed our forests of sandalwood. They destroyed our people and tried to destroy our gods. Our way of life was *pau*. Finished. At last our great king died, for even though he was like a god, he was mortal and death came for him too.

"After his death, his beloved wife Queen Kaahumanu, and his weak son Liholiho, and Liholiho's mother destroyed *kapu*. They ate together in public, the man and the women, and the women ate *kapu* foods—they ate bananas and coconut and pork." His face grew stern, recalling the horrible sacrilege committed some 180 years ago. "If the rulers do not keep the rules, how can the people know what to do?"

"The missionaries came and the whalers came and our people started to die. Our culture started to die and our religion lost its power. Our people stopped listening to the gods, and the gods stopped listening to our prayers. We have tried to preserve our traditions. It is not finished! It is not *pau*!" He exclaimed explosively, shoving his fist at the sun.

Then he took a deep breath and let it out slowly. "Now we must prepare for the ceremony. We must cleanse ourselves in the sea."

He paused, then continued. "In the old days, Noa Noa, you would not be allowed to watch unless you prayed with us. But you do not know the prayers, and, besides, times have changed. I believe you have a good heart, even though you are ignorant of our ways. You may watch, but you must not speak."

The *kahuna* and his granddaughter went down to the beach and appeared to splash themselves with salt water. He stood for a moment, hands upraised, apparently praying, then he walked slowly back to the ruined temple. Melemele disappeared behind a lava outcrop. When she returned she was wearing what looked like a bathing suit top and the tapa-cloth skirt. On her wrists were ruffled bands of greenery; around her ankles were bone and shell bands that rattled as she walked.

Turning to face the sea, the *kahuna* began to beat a complex rhythm on the *ipu*, a rhythm that seemed to ebb and flow with the lapping of the waves on the black-sand beach a few yards away. Soon he began to chant a strangely compelling song whose lyrics I could not understand but whose ancient meaning seemed beyond words, spilling out of the sounds themselves and merging with the air, the earth, and the ocean.

Beautiful Melemele faced the sea and began to move, instantly embodying the chant in motion, her graceful hands inscribing complex shapes in the air, her body swaying to the beat of the *ipu*, the pounding of the surf, the shape of the words.

The ceremony ended abruptly. At least, the ending seemed abrupt to me, though I suppose they knew it was coming. Even after the chanting ceased, I still felt it throbbing in the air around me.

The *kahuna* put down the calabash, and Melemele stood motionless, staring out to sea. With a deep sigh, she turned towards me, eyes blurred with tears. Then she walked over to the pink nylon bag and took out a small, leaf-wrapped bundle. She placed it in the middle of the stone altar.

The *kahuna* said, "It is done. *Pau.*"

She nodded and took off her leafy adornments and dropped them on the altar, too. Wiping her eyes, she picked up the calabash and placed it back in the bag; then she disappeared behind a rock outcropping, presumably to change clothes.

David said, "You go now. We will follow soon."

I nodded solemnly and started back up the trail, wondering what secret rituals they would complete now that the *wahine haole*—or should that be *haole wahine*—was out of sight. Soon they and the ancient temple were hidden behind the twisted piles of lava. A helicopter buzzed overhead, perhaps on a sightseeing tour of Haleakala crater, complete with personalized video souvenir. I saw a tiny nearby island that had not been visible from the beach by the hotel.

A large double-hulled motorboat roared by.

Suddenly a man jumped out from behind a pile of lava and grabbed me from behind, one nicotine-drenched hand pressed hard over my mouth, one arm wrapped tightly around my waist.

I couldn't see who it was, but I knew it was male. As he tried to drag me down the trail, I fought, kicking and struggling, at every step. One particularly vicious stomp connected to his instep.

"Shit!" he exclaimed, as he instinctively loosened his grip around my mouth.

I managed to jerk my head free and scream. I also looked down. I recognized those shiny black shoes. It was Joe.

He tried to cover my mouth again, but this time I was ready. I chomped down on his finger and, as he howled in pain, I broke loose and ran back down the trail towards the temple. After a moment's delay, I could hear Joe coming close behind, his shoes crunching loudly on the lava cinders.

I rounded a bend in the trail and skidded into David and Melemele. Joe took one look at the *kahuna* and turned and fled.

Gasping for breath, I exclaimed, "He attacked me!"

Startled, David looked up, as if coming out of a daze. Melemele started to turn back.

Just then a shot rang out and David fell to the ground. Melemele and I dropped prone beside him.

He lay still, breathing heavily. Blood streamed from his arm and turned his faded Aloha shirt red.

"Are you badly hurt?" I whispered.

"No," he replied stoically, "It is just a scratch."

"Are you sure, Grandfather?" Melemele asked, voice trembling.

"I am sure. It is too bad my martial arts are of no use against bullets."

"What could they want?" I asked.

"What do you think?"

"The *tiki?*"

He nodded.

"How could they know I have it with me?" I asked.

Lying on his side, he managed to shrug his shoulders.

Melemele started to stand up, but he pulled her down, scraping her legs on the sharp cinders.

"Do not stand up," he ordered. "You make a good target."

Melemele whimpered softly. Another bullet whizzed by, shattering a cairn of lava next to us. Suddenly there was a burst of gunfire, seemingly coming from all directions at once.

I admit it. I cowered, arms covering my head, covering my ears, pressing my body flat into the sharp-edged lava. I couldn't get low enough. If I had had my cell phone, I could have called the police. If there'd been a signal out here in the middle of nowhere. If. If. If.

Just then I heard someone coming from behind, whistling. It was the lone fisherman we had seen earlier. He was obviously surprised to find three people lying flat in the middle of the path, and even more surprised to see blood staining David's arm.

"Waddascoops, brah?" He asked nervously.

"Some lolo buggah shootin' at us!" David whispered.

"Shootin'? You sure?"

"Of course he's sure!" I snapped.

"I don't hear nothin'," he replied.

He was right. The shooting had stopped. Perhaps the sight of a stranger had frightened them off.

David sat up, wiping the blood off his arm. The wound was shallow, and the bleeding had almost stopped.

"I think we should go," he said calmly.

Cautiously, we stood up and waited for the renewed whizzing of bullets, the crash of splintered lava, the heavy thudding impact of bullet in flesh. Nothing happened.

"Don't you think we should wait a while?" I suggested.

"They have fled," David replied.

"Why would they run away so soon?" I asked.

Again he shrugged. "Maybe the fisherman frightened them away."

Slowly, cautiously, jumping at every unexpected sound, the four of us walked single-file back to our car. In the distance we could see a cloud of white exhaust billowing from behind a retreating vehicle, but it was too far away to tell the make or model.

The fisherman eyed us cautiously but made no effort to leave.

Looking around, I realized there was no other vehicle parked at the trailhead.

"Do you want a ride?" I asked him hesitantly.

With a leery smile, he replied, "No 'tanks, brah. You got da'kine trouble. I gonna walk." And he headed down the trail in front of us, whistling as he went.

Nine

The three of us watched the retreating fisherman in silence, then turned to each other.

"Well," I said, with false cheer, "What do we do now?"

David gazed out to sea for a minute before replying. "We think about what has happened. We are safe here, for the moment."

Melemele protested, "I gotta get to work soon, Grandfather."

"We will stay here and think," he commanded sternly.

He walked over to a nearby tidal pool and squatted on the ground, holding his injured arm a bit stiffly. Melemele, graceful as always, folded like a flower next to him and stared off into space. I sat cross-legged on the other side, staring in fascination at the odd assortment of spiky, crawly creatures scuttling around in the shallow water.

David breathed deeply for a moment, then said, "We must learn where the *tikis* were hidden. Noa, have you remembered anything that might help us?"

"Don't you think we should just go home? And the sooner the better?"

He looked at me sternly. "We must not weaken. There is no safety in surrender, Noa. There is only cowardice."

I nodded. He was right. There was no way through this but to keep on going through this. The sooner we found the *tikis* the better off we would be. We might actually get out of this alive, though I had my doubts.

"You must try to remember, Noa."

Shaking my head, I said, "I don't remember anything. Unless," I continued hesitantly, "I don't know if this means anything, but Alex told me about the nude beach at Makena, and he promised to show it to me. He said it was one of his favorite spots on the island."

Aloha exclaimed, "He told me he never went there! Why would he want to take you there?"

"Maybe he was joking," I said, trying to soothe her.

"Maybe so. He liked to joke a lot," she conceded.

"This talk about Makena Beach may be important," David replied. "Maybe Alex hid the *tikis* there. Let us go." He started to stand up.

"Before we leave, David, I want to ask you a question," I said somewhat stiffly.

"Yes?"

"Why did Sam and Joe try to shoot us?"

"Because they want the *tiki*," David replied.

"But how did they know I had it?" I asked, trying hard not to sound as suspicious as I felt.

"Maybe someone told them. Or they saw you with Alex."

Maybe, I thought. Maybe. But who could have told them? Bill Miller? And why shoot at us? I might have been killed. Wouldn't they want to know where the other *tikis* were before they killed me? Of course, someone, probably them, had killed Alex before finding out where the *tikis* were hidden, so why assume they had gotten any smarter?

Questions scurried around in my mind like the creatures in the tidal pool. How did they know where to find us? Was it pure luck they had followed us to this isolated part of the island, or had they had advance warning? And why had Melemele and David stayed behind and sent me on ahead down the path? Was it merely by chance that Joe had caught me alone?

My head was spinning from the possibilities, and I could see no clear answers. A line from a song kept running through my head: "Who do you trust? Tell me, who do you trust?"

Cautiously, I ventured, "I think we should tell the police."

David shook his head emphatically. "The police will not help you. They do not believe you."

I had to admit that, so far, he was right about that. The police had been anything but helpful. Still, I had to try to convince him, as much for his sake as for mine. "But the police have to believe us now. You've been shot. That should be proof of something, don't you think?"

He said, "The police cannot protect us. And they cannot help us find the *tikis*. We must find them. We must not let anything stop us!" He stared at me intently. "You have shared in our sacred rites. It is now your duty to help us."

I could tell he'd been hanging out with anthropologists. He knew just what buttons to push.

He continued, "The *tikis* are all we have left. They are the last link to our ancient greatness. They are the gods of the great King Kamehameha. If they are taken from the island and sold to some foreigner, the power that is still here on this island will be gone. We will dwindle away until we are no more."

It was like handing candy to a baby, all this talk of dying cultures and ancient wrongs. After all, I'm an anthropologist—how could I refuse to help? Besides, I'd rather help the *kahuna* of my own free will than be forced at gunpoint to help the two goons.

David cradled his arm gently and winced, involuntarily, as he stood up. As we walked back to the car, I noticed a trail of tiny, glistening spatters on the ground.

"Look!" I pointed to the shiny red drops.

David bent down, touched a drop, and smelled it. "It is blood."

"But whose?"

He looked at me questioningly.

"Somebody shot you, and we heard gunfire," I said thoughtfully. "But how could the people firing at us have gotten wounded?"

Shrugging his shoulders, David replied, "Perhaps they slipped on the lava when they made their getaway."

"Maybe so," I said.

Watching on all sides for ambushes, we headed out of the lava flow and back to the main highway.

Lost in thought, I almost missed the turnoff for Makena Beach. David warned me just in time, and I took a sharp turn onto the rutted dirt road. Several other cars were parked in the sandy clearing next to the trail. We could only hope that none of them was Sam and Joe's. We didn't know what we were looking for, but Alex had mentioned nude bathing at Makena Beach. It was all we had to go on.

Cautiously, we walked through the forest of *koa, kiawe,* and cactuses until we reached a wide stretch of white sand beach. In the distance was the same island I had seen from the King's Trail.

Pointing at it, I asked David, "What's that?"

With a frown, he replied, "That is Kaho'olawe, a sacred island born to Wakea and Papa. It is the island of Kanaloa, the man-god who was driven from heaven by Kane, the god of light. Kanaloa ruled over all poisonous things and over the land of the dead." He continued angrily, "For generations our people lived and worshipped on the island. Then your government took it from us. For a while, nothing lived on the sacred land except a band of wild goats. The land was scarred with bomb craters."

I looked at him in shock. "Bomb craters?"

"Your Navy used it for target practice. They desecrated the sacred land. They bombed it, turning it into a barren wasteland. We asked for the land back, but nothing happened. Then we began to use *haole* tactics. We filed a lawsuit. It took more than 20 years, but we got Kaho'olawe back, and the Navy had to restore the land and protect the sacred sites." His eyes looked far away. "Unlike your government, we believe in *Aloha aina*."

"What's that?"

"Love of the land."

"I thought *Aloha* was a greeting—that it meant 'hello' or 'goodbye.'"

"*Aloha* means those things, but it also means 'love,'" he explained patiently. "*Aina* means 'land.' '*Aloha aina*' means love of the land. It means that we recognize that the land and the ocean around Kaho'olawe is a living spiritual being. We respect it and are its caretakers."

Aloha explained, "Grandfather belongs to Protect Kaho'olawe 'Ohana. They fought the Navy for years until they won."

"Do you belong, too?" I asked, curious to learn more about her.

She shook her head, voice tense. "I got other things to do."

To the left was Big Beach, where several sunbathers dozed in the sun. It was obvious at a glance that none of them was a gun-toting insurance investigator. To the right was a narrow rocky path, which we followed around a 360-foot-high red cinder cone to the sandy, secluded cove called Pu'u Ola'i or Little Beach.

I must admit I was nervous—and not because we had just been shot at. I'd never been to a nudist beach.

No one was there. Or to be more precise, there was no one on the beach, although half a dozen snorkelers were bobbing around in the water offshore. It was impossible to tell if they were nude or not.

We scoured the forested edge of the beach, peering under the thorn-filled *kiawe* trees, but there were no freshly dug mounds, no newly disturbed sand. There was nothing to indicate where Alex had hidden the *tikis*—if, in fact, he had hidden them there. After half an hour, we gave up in frustration.

"It seems that the 'Aloha Spirit' is not with us," David said.

"'Aloha Spirit'? Why do you say that?" I asked, as something tickled the edge of memory.

"The Aloha Spirit is many things. It is the spirit of Hawaii. Friendliness, understanding, love, good luck . . . .."

"Alex used that expression a lot. He kept talking about 'the Aloha Spirit.' And then he'd laugh a little."

"We used to talk about it, too," Melemele said, her voice tinged with sadness. "In fact, we had a favorite spot in Haleakala that we called 'the place of the Aloha Spirit.' Alex said it was a very holy place."

"I told him about that place," David said thoughtfully.

"We went there a few times," Melemele remembered. "Alex told me it was important to go there together, so we went."

I was getting excited. "Maybe he hid the *tikis* there. After all, what better place to hide sacred figures than in a sacred place?"

David nodded. "Let us go."

"I don't suppose it would have been safe to hide something here anyway," I muttered, glancing around at the exposed beach and the possibly exposed snorkelers.

"You are right. Too many people visit the beach."

With cheeriness I didn't really feel, I said, "On to Haleakala!"

Melemele interrupted nervously, "It's getting late. I've got to rehearse for the *luau* tomorrow night."

"You perform in a *luau*, too?" I asked in surprise, then recalled David had mentioned that earlier.

"Yes."

"Where?"

"At the Royal Princess."

"But I thought that was on Friday night," I said, remembering that Alex and I had had watched the *luau* dancers from the balcony of the Aloha restaurant.

"Friday and Monday," Melemele replied, then started down the path to the car.

Thoughtfully, I followed slowly behind. Had Melemele seen Alex and me leaning on the restaurant railing, looking chummy? Had she been overcome with jealousy and, not satisfied with his explanation, killed him the next morning? She looked delicate, but she was a dancer—she was healthy and strong, strong enough, presumably, to bash someone—especially a cheating lover—in the head with a stone. Add one more to the list of suspects.

We dropped Melemele off at the Royal Princess, then stopped at the Maui Surfside to get warm clothes. The temperature at the top of the crater could be 30° colder than at sea level, David warned me.

The light on the telephone was flashing when I got to my room. A message. I called the operator. There were three messages: one from Robert Wiley, asking me to call; one from Bill Miller, hoping to meet me in the lobby for dinner at 7 p.m.; and one from Nestor Mendoza, ordering me to call him as soon as possible.

I had thought about calling the police to report the attempted kidnapping despite David's resistance, but my antipathy to Nestor and his orders overrode the urge. Besides, there wasn't time. David was waiting. I could always call later.

Since I had flown in from New York I had a winter coat, hat, and gloves with me. I bundled them up, along with a blanket, and headed back to the car.

"Which way?" I asked.

"Towards Kihei, then towards the airport at Kahului."

Surprised, I said, "You mean we have to go half-way around the island? Isn't there a shorter way?" Of course, since the island at its largest dimensions is only about 40 miles east to west and 25 miles north to south, and the isthmus is only about 7 miles across, even half-way wasn't too far.

He shook his head. "There is an upcountry road only a few miles from where we were at Makena, but it ends without connecting to the highway."

That was typical of the island, I realized. Maui was shaped like a misshapen figure eight lying on its side, but no road went all the way around either loop. The tour driver on the Road to Hana had explained the natives liked their privacy, and if either loop were completed, there would be no place safe from tourists. He was undoubtedly right.

One result of this lack of completion, however, was that the few "belt" roads that existed were overcrowded, coming and going, and traffic jams in paradise were occurring more and more frequently. Still, it was oddly reassuring to realize that greed and tourist dollars hadn't reached everywhere on Maui.

"How long will this take?"

"About two hours each way, plus we must walk into the crater to the place of the Aloha Spirit."

I glanced at my watch; it was nearly noon. This lost *tiki* business was playing havoc with my eating schedule.

"I want to stop somewhere and get something to eat before heading up to the crater," I said.

"We will pass by a good place to buy lunch. I will tell you."

We drove north on Kihei road, passing one small shopping mall after another. Kentucky Fried Chicken. McDonalds. IHOP. Prime Rib House. DQ. Mexican Cafe. All You Can Eat Smorgasbord. New York Deli. Lappert's Gourmet Ice Cream Store. WikiWiki Pizza. At last David signaled, and I turned into the Paradise Food Shop parking lot. Nobody seemed to be following us.

While David waited in the car, I entered the ramshackle building and stepped right into a barely updated version of a 1960s California health-food bar. A chalkboard over the deli counter advertised an eclectic assortment of daily specials, including a tofu and Maui-onion salad and a sprouts-tomato-pepper-cheese-on-whole-wheat sandwich, as well as a mouthwatering selection of carob cookies and wheat germ desserts. A nearby bulletin board displayed help wanted and employment sought ads, housing opportunities, and a variety of (to me) encoded messages.

The clientele was as diverse as the menu, though heavily weighted towards beach bums and New Age types. Sometimes it was hard to tell the difference. Most were young, blond, tan, wearing tie-dyed T-shirts, neon shorts, one dangling peace-sign earring, and braided friendship bracelets and anklets. There were also burned-out old men, vacant-eyed middle-aged ones, cheery young women, and one elderly gray-haired lady in an old-fashioned, ankle-length muumuu with pineapple appliqués around the hem.

With an effort, I controlled my fascination and did what I had come to do: buy lunch. After surveying the contents of several refrigerator cases, I selected a fairly tame vegetarian sandwich for David and, for me, a Chinese-take-out-style carton, the same they used to put goldfish in at the dime store, full of something called vegetarian fried chicken. A couple of oranges, a few bananas from the open fruit bins, two bottles of unfiltered guaranteed natural passion fruit/mango juice, and a slice of carrot cake completed the feast.

After waiting in line for what seemed like an unnecessarily long time, listening to someone trying to work a deal to sell it wasn't clear what, and to a vague description of some strange doings upcountry, I made my purchases and ran out to the car. Between the street slang and the *pidgin* lingo, I had understood little. David was waiting patiently.

Eating as we went—the cold faux-fried-chicken tofu strips were actually finger-licking good but greasy—we soon left Kihei and turned onto the Puunene highway, driving through fields of sugarcane screened behind dense tree-like bushes. At one point, acrid, caramel-smelling smoke billowed across the road and a flagman waved us to a halt.

"They burn the cane before harvest," David explained. "The trees help stop the smoke, but they don't stop very much of it."

Driving slowly, we edged our way forward and out of the burn zone. Further down the road we reached the Alexander & Baldwin Sugar museum. The Puunene sugar mill across the street looked like a Rube Goldberg contraption of tall green smoke stacks, huge conveyor belts, oil-drenched cranes, flashing lights, and assorted Quonset huts. Just past Puunene, we turned off onto another road and drove through more sugar cane fields, wending our way slowly through the village of Pukalani to Rt. 377, the Haleakala Highway. Driving six miles further "upcountry"—a state of mind as much as a direction, according to tourist brochures—we reached the zigzag of Rt. 378, the Haleakala Crater Road. Some 22 miles further, we arrived at the summit.

In 38 miles the narrow road twisted its way up from sea level to 10,023 feet, supposedly the shortest road to climb that high in the world. Or so the road sign boasted. We drove out of the sugarcane fields, through tropical rainforests, past California-style houses surrounded by six-foot-tall poinsettia hedges, through the land of cactuses and cattle, and into the land of shaggy-barked eucalyptus and pine-tree forests. Horses grazed behind white picket fences, and groves of towering *koa* trees alternated with stands of graceful Norfolk pines. And that was just the first 6,000 feet or so.

From sea level Haleakala didn't look that high because the slope is so gentle, but as we wove back and forth, back and forth up the side of the volcano, it kept looking higher and higher. It also got distinctly cooler. Soon the verdant slopes were left behind, as were the trees.

As I rounded one tight corner, I was suddenly confronted by a flock of downhill bicyclists, all wearing identical helmets, gloves, and yellow and blue wind gear. The front rider appeared to be the leader; he was wearing a safety vest and glancing around frequently to check on the bicyclists behind him. Bringing up the rear was a color coordinated van—Ridin' Rick's Audacious Adventures. I drove by cautiously, afraid one of the bicyclists might suddenly lose control and fall.

David explained, "Several tour groups take people up by van to the top of the crater; then they bicycle down."

"Is it safe?" I asked, doubtfully.

"I have never gone. But they use special bikes, with heavy-duty brakes. I've heard it is hard on the hands and wrists because you have to brake all the time."

"No accounting for taste," I muttered, clenching the steering wheel tightly. I hate heights. I don't jump off the high dive at the pool; I don't go parasailing or hang gliding; I don't bicycle down mountains. I was having a difficult enough time driving up Haleakala. The thought of what it would be like driving down, on the outside edge of the narrow winding asphalt strip, filled me with dread. At least on the way up I was driving towards the mountain or on the mountainside of the road most of the time, so I only occasionally caught a glimpse of the awe-inspiring vista unfolding below. My hands started to sweat. I wiped them off on my clothes.

I tried to remember my relaxation exercises: breathe in, breathe out. Why was it that driving up and back down a mountain terrified me more than getting shot at?

Dense patches of fog suddenly materialized, making it hard to see the road—fortunately, the fog also blocked off the impressive—but terrifying—view of the sea and the isthmus far below.

After what seemed like much too long, we reached the park headquarters. 7,000 feet elevation. Ten more road miles to go to the summit. From where we were, it didn't look that far to the top. I guess the perspective flattened the distance. I pulled off to go to the restroom. Anxiety does that to me.

Planted alongside the headquarters were some silverswords, one of the world's rarest plants, according to the botanical label. The plant was shaped like a huge spiked ball, but at the end of its five-to twenty-year life, it sprouts a six-foot-tall stalk of hundreds of purplish-red flowers, then withers into a gaunt, gray skeleton. Talk about going out with a bang. Fuzzy blue hairs covered the sage-green sword-like leaves, protecting them from the sun's radiation and helping them retain moisture. The silversword reminded me of a century plant, though it is actually a distant relative of the sunflower.

Further on, we drove by a puzzling sign: "*Nene* crossing." I didn't have long to wait before finding out what it meant. Several cars had pulled over to the side of the road, and passengers were spilling out to take photos of a brown-and-white goose with a corkscrew-striped neck. It posed obligingly, letting out a low moaning sound instead of a honk. This was a *nene*, Hawaii's state bird, a distant descendant of a pair—at least—of Canadian geese, blown off-course centuries ago, who then adapted to life on the rim of Haleakala.

We had left the tree line far below, but we still had quite a distance to go. A few hardy bushes sprouted out of the reddish-black, decomposing volcanic rock face from which the road had been blasted.

Trying to make conversation, I asked, "Why do they call the volcano Haleakala?" I knew by now that most Hawaiian names meant something.

Coming back from wherever he was mentally traveling, David answered, after a delay, "It means 'House of the Sun.' It is here at the summit that the demigod Maui lassoed the sun and commanded it to slow down in its journey across the sky so that his mother would have time to finish her chores while it was still daylight. The mountain is a very sacred, powerful place. It is the home of Madame Pele."

"Madame Pele?"

"The goddess of volcanoes. She has flaming red hair and glowing eyes. Those who have seen her say she is very beautiful."

He lapsed back into silence.

We drove by another sign—"Turn on headlights in clouds." Now I was sure we were higher than I wanted to be. We drove by two overlooks, but I passed them up; I'd just as soon not know what I was missing. David didn't seem to notice. He sat silent, withdrawn, staring out the window.

At the end of the road was a huge parking lot filled with tour buses and rental cars. As I stepped out of the car a strong gust of chilly wind nearly knocked me off my feet. Quickly, I put on my coat and hat and stuffed my gloves in my pockets. David draped himself in the blanket. He looked like a dignified Indian chief.

"Where to?" I asked, as the wind took my words and blew them away.

He pointed towards a trailhead near the visitors' center.

Buffeted by the wind, I yelled, "Before we start down the trail, I want to take a few minutes to see the exhibits." After all, I realized, this would probably be my only chance to see Haleakala and, by God, I was determined to do some proper sight-seeing on this island.

David nodded. Blanket flapping in the breeze, he led the way.

According to the elaborate three-dimensional displays, Haleakala is the world's largest dormant volcano. There are two main types of lava, I read, and Haleakala contains them both. A'a—what we'd seen at the King's Trail—spews out partly solid and filled with gasses, then breaks apart to form clinkers. Pahoehoe lava, the hottest natural substance on earth, flows in swift, fiery rivers and solidifies into a smooth surface, somewhat like hardened pancake batter—successive layers had formed the gently sloping shell of the volcano.

Haleakala extends 20,000 feet or so under the sea, as well as more than 10,000 feet above. The highest spot on Maui is 10,023 feet, at Puu'ulaula, a short uphill climb from the parking lot. At the very top is a glass-encased observation deck—to help keep visitors from being blown off, I suppose. The wind howls fiercely at the top of the world.

Over the millennia, the volcano has lost several thousand feet in height, and erosion has formed the bowl-shaped crater. The crater itself is 3,000 feet deep, 7.5 miles long, and 2.5 miles wide—19 square miles in all, with a circumference of 21 miles. It could hold the city of Manhattan.

The volcano's incredible mass as it rises over 30,000 feet makes it one of the densest on earth, and its gravitational pull is staggering. So maybe the old *kahunas* were right about the awesome power of the place. New Agers certainly think so; they come to the crater in droves.

Looking out through the observation window I saw nothing but clouds, spilling out two torn sides of the crater. Suddenly they cleared away, revealing the crater itself—a breathtaking moonscape of overlapping mounds and hollows and great vacant stretches, in shifting shades of crimson and rust and ocher and mauve and yellow, immense rigid piles of fused clinkers, enormous shifting dunes of lava ash. No wonder the astronauts trained there before landing on the moon. Ant-size hikers were visible far below, following pale, twisting trails to the bottom of the crater.

A line of what appeared to be nine little hillocks crossed the floor. According to the topological map, they were actually a mini mountain range and each was a volcanic vent, with a high iron content. The smallest cinder cone was 600 feet high, the tallest 1,000.

The crater was deceptive. It didn't look that big. None of it—not the rim, not the cinder cones—looked that big. Or that deep. It was awesome.

The clouds swept back in, blanketing the crater again and tendrils of mist wafted up like smoke.

David said, "We had better go. We have a long walk ahead of us."

Taking a deep breath, which was a bit hard to do in the thin air, I followed him down the Shifting Sands trail.

Once we got below the rim of the crater, the force of the wind was broken and it was actually a bit warmer. In fact, it was too warm, once the clouds cleared off again. Changeable as luck, the weather shifted from bitter cold to rainy to blistering hot. And back. Not a user-friendly environment.

I try to stay fit, but I'm not very good at it. It's not that I lack discipline, it's just that I lack time. At any rate, hiking at 10,000 feet is not easy, and keeping up with David was extremely difficult. He marched rapidly along, seemingly as unstressed as if he were strolling on a beach at sea level.

The crater was spooky. Silent. Arid. Drifting dunes of volcanic sand giving way to raw-edged mounds of fused lava cinders that looked as if they had been carved with a blowtorch or churned out of rust-colored cement.

The rattle of displaced cinders rolling down the slope startled me; I spun around and saw not a would-be kidnapper but a wild mountain goat. I breathed a sigh of relief.

I heard footsteps and turned nervously to see who was coming up behind me. It was a young couple, complete with backpacks, hiking boots, and walking sticks. Behind them came a group of chattering Japanese tourists wearing large plastic garbage bags with holes cut in them for their heads and arms—creative outfitting to break the wind and insulate against the cold. David stepped off the trail and let the parade pass by. Then he turned to me.

"In the ancient days, *kahunas* brought their apprentices here for initiation. There were good healing *kahunas* and dangerous black sorcerers, and they battled mightily for power on top of Haleakala. Only *kahunas* and their apprentices could live here, and even they could not stay very long. It is a place too full of energy."

Turning abruptly, he headed off on a narrow trail towards a nearby cinder cone. I followed. Without breaking stride, he began to climb up the side, carefully avoiding the isolated silverswords.

"Where are we going?" I puffed.

He pointed towards the top. "This is the place of the Aloha Spirit."

Breathing rapidly, trying not to hyperventilate, I struggled along behind him. He got there before me and disappeared inside. I turned to look back up the trail; nobody had followed us. I climbed in after.

It was a very odd place. Strangely sensuous, the curving sides formed a gently sloping bowl, filled with shadows and fissures. A few Ti-leaf bundles next to a cinder cairn confirmed we were not the first to come here in search of something, though we wanted to take something away, not leave it behind.

My legs felt oddly shaky, and the hair on the back of my neck stood up. Electrical charge? Power points? Altitude sickness? I didn't have any idea. All I knew was I wanted out.

The *kahuna*, however, was completely at ease. He carefully explored the extensive cinder-covered surface, looking for a hiding place for the *tikis*. I made a desultory effort to do the same but found it very hard to concentrate.

Far from feeling protected by the enclosing walls, I felt claustrophobic and very, very nervous. Even the air smelled strange, a combination of sulfur and rust. Shades of Lucifer or, maybe, Hades. With a shiver, I realized I was breathing in the very breath of the volcano, emanating from the enormously ancient, molten center of the earth.

I didn't belong there and I wanted out.

At last David completed his circumambulation. Shaking his head in frustration, he said, "The *tikis* are not here. I would know. They were never here."

As if in response, the cinder cone seemed to belch. Pale threads of gas started rising from the fissures at the bottom. I had been feeling increasingly light-headed for some time; now I suddenly became extremely ill. My vision began to blur, and I sat down abruptly, not even feeling the sharp-edged cinders, then toppled over. David moved towards me in slow motion.

"We must leave now," he said faintly, and then collapsed beside me.

A dream-like phantom-figure with flaming red hair appeared out of nowhere and moved towards me.

The next thing I knew, I was stretched out on the rim of the cinder cone, gasping for air. My clothes stank of sulfur and my head ached. David was lying next to me. Soon he began to sit up.

"What happened?" I asked groggily.

Shaking his head, David replied, "I do not know. Perhaps we offended Madame Pele."

"But how did we get out of the cinder cone?"

"Someone must have carried us out."

"But where are they? Why did they leave?"

"Maybe they did not want to be seen," he said slowly. "Maybe it was the *menehune*."

"The who?"

"The *menehune*. The little people. They are like your Irish leprechauns. They do not like to be seen, and they rarely go out in daylight."

From my perch atop the cinder cone, I surveyed the area. Nobody was near. Maybe David was right. It was as good an explanation as any, I supposed, and probably more likely than my fiery-haired hallucination.

We hurried back down the trail and then, laboriously, climbed back up to the parking lot. Now all I had to do was drive down 10,000 feet to the distant sea.

I don't want to talk about it except to say we made it down safely. Despite the snow. Yes, snow. It is a rare occurrence, and it doesn't last for long, but it happens: big wet flakes fell on the rough lava slope and coated the black asphalt road with a slick, wet glaze. Snow turned to rain, and in the distance a rainbow arched across the sky.

We got down. It took a long time, most of it in low gear. Drivers blew their horns impatiently, and I pulled over frequently to let them pass. But there was always more traffic coming up behind.

At last we made it back to horizontality and the sugarcane fields. Maybe the *kahuna* had said a silent prayer.

Ten

When I got back to my room, the message light on the phone was blinking again. Nestor had called and demanded that I call him back ASAP. It was 6:30 p.m., and I was supposed to meet Bill at 7:00. Although I wanted to relax for a few minutes, bathe, and change clothes, I didn't want to give the police any excuses for considering me a hostile witness. If they only knew.

So I called Nestor.

"This is Noa Webster, returning your call."

"Where've you been? We've been worried—"

"Worried?" I said, surprised by the subtle difference in tone.

"Yeah, worried," he growled. "It's not good for tourism if tourists get hurt on Maui."

That sounded more like Nestor.

"We got a report that somebody had been shot out at the lava flow."

"You mean the fisherman called the police?" I said, surprised.

"That's right. The description fit you and that *kahuna* you mentioned. Anybody get hurt?" he demanded.

"David was hurt a little, but not much."

"What happened? Go slow. Tell me the details."

I took a deep breath. "This morning the *kahuna* invited me to go sightseeing with him."

"To the lava flow?"

"It's actually quite fascinating. A nice change from all this tropical greenery. Besides, he and his granddaughter wanted to go to the old *heiau* at the end of the trail."

"I know it. I've been there."

"You've been there?" I said, surprised.

"Why not? I've lived here all my life. You get to know the island pretty well after that much time. Besides, my girlfriend's a native Hawaiian."

"Your girlfriend? But I thought—" I blurted.

"I know what Larry told you." His voice grew gruff, "But we're not talking about me, we're talking about you. So start at the beginning."

"Two guys—they claimed to be insurance investigators but I don't think they were—came to my room early this morning and frightened me, but David scared them away."

"What was the *kahuna* doing there?"

"Not what you think!"

"Give me a break, Noa. I apologize for yesterday, okay? I'm really a decent guy. Even cops have bad days. We're only human."

I started to make a snide reply but stopped. "David just happened to stop by and scared them away. They said they'd get even. I think one of them had a gun."

There was a moment of silence. "A gun?"

"Well, he was wearing a jacket and he started to put his hand inside . . ."

"Right," he said, skeptically.

"Anyway, he said he'd get even. And then, as we were coming back from the *heiau*, Joe jumped out at me—"

"Joe?"

"The short, balding one. But I got away. And then somebody—it must have been Sam—shot the *kahuna* in the arm."

"Whoa. You're going too fast. Who's Sam?"

"The other insurance agent. At least, that's what he said his name was. Or what Joe said his name was. I don't remember, now."

"So you're telling me that two guys tried to muscle their way into your room this morning and you think one of them had a gun. And then the *kahuna* just happened to come along—"

It had seemed fortuitous at the time, not suspicious.

"And scared them away. And then you went sightseeing with the *kahuna* and his granddaughter, and one of the insurance agents tried to kidnap you or mug you but you escaped. And the other one shot David." He paused for a moment. "Have I got this straight?"

"You got it." I decided to skip Haleakala and the *menehune*. With a sigh, I realized that even I didn't find that story very believable, so how could I expect Nestor to believe it?

"You know, you are more trouble . . . ." Nestor complained.

Angrily, I replied, "Look, Mr. Mendoza, I came to Maui to have a vacation and to present a paper at a conference. So far, my vacation has been much less than satisfactory. Exciting, perhaps, but not a lot of fun. I finally get to do some sightseeing, and someone tries to kidnap me and my companion gets shot. How do you think I feel about it!" I was getting quite worked up. "If this is how sympathetic you are, no wonder your girlfriend left you!"

There was a moment of silence.

"Okay, okay," Nestor said. I could almost picture him raising his hands in surrender.

"I get shot at," I continued, fueled by righteous anger, "And you act like it's my fault!"

"Calm down, will you?" Nestor said placatingly. "Now listen, Dr. Webster, you got a point. No doubt about it. I'm sorry we didn't trust you at the beginning. But your story gets weirder all the time, so I guess it must be true. Nobody could make this up."

"Thanks—I think—for the vote of confidence. If that's what it was."

"Truce?"

"Truce." I agreed, then looked at my watch. "I have to go. I've got a dinner date."

"May I ask who with?"

"Bill Miller."

"The guy you saw last night?"

"I'm warning you!"

"Don't be so defensive. Just wanted to make sure I got it straight for the record. The name sounds familiar."

"He says he's an art dealer from California. Look, it's been great, but I got to go."

"Before you hang up, tell me how to get hold of the *kahuna* and the girl. I need to talk to them."

"I don't know."

"You don't know?" He said, disbelief thick in his voice.

"I really don't know. The *kahuna* shows up when he feels like, then he disappears."

"Of course he does," he said soothingly.

"But I know the *kahuna*'s last name. I wrote it down." I found the cocktail napkin in my purse. "Kukuilani. David Kukuilani."

"Thanks. Look—promise me if anything happens you'll call me. Or if you find out how to reach them. Okay? I won't hassle you. I won't make you come in for a statement if you promise."

"Okay. It's a deal."

"Take down this number."

I did. "What number is it?"

"My home. And here's my cell phone, but the coverage is pretty bad on the island. Remember. Call me any time," he said, then paused, then added, almost as an afterthought, "By the way, anything more about the *tiki*?"

"What *tiki*?" I said, then hung up.

No time to relax. No time for a shower, even though I stank of sulfur. Barely time to change clothes and purses. Just as I started to leave the room, the phone rang, so I turned back to answer it. I'm compulsive that way—I will leap, dripping, slipping from the shower to lunge for the phone. As if it were a once-in-a-lifetime opportunity. As if they wouldn't call back. As if.

"Hello, Noa."

"Peter?" I gasped.

"Who else?"

"It's great to hear your voice!"

"Yours too, love."

"What's up?"

"In the interest of decency, my dear—"

Laughing, I said, "What I meant was, why'd you call?"

"An overwhelming longing to hear your dulcet tones. Besides, I have good news: I've changed my plans. I'll arrive in Maui on Tuesday at 3:00 p.m. on American Airlines. Isn't that patriotic?"

"How uncharacteristic!"

He laughed. "It was the best connection I could find. Can you pick me up?"

If I'm still alive, I thought. "Delighted to, Peter! But what happened? I thought you weren't coming till later."

"London's cold and dreary, the company is tedious, and the relatives are getting on my nerves. So I thought to myself, thought I, why should I waste the precious moments of my life in foul weather?"

"Oh," I said, feeling somewhat disappointed.

"Besides, I'd rather be with you."

"Ah. How nice of you to say that," I replied, slightly stiffly.

"After all, there you are, basking in the sun, enjoying all sorts of tropical delights—"

"Hah!" I replied. "Little do you know."

"Trouble in paradise?"

"You said it."

"Surely not," he groaned.

"Indeed. Murder, mayhem—"

"Start at the beginning," he demanded, "but keep it brief."

"I don't have time to talk anyway. Suffice it to say a man I met was murdered and the police suspect me."

"Why?"

"Why what? Why murdered? Or why me?"

"Don't fence with me, Noa," he replied, irritated.

"Funny you should use that expression." I hesitated, wondering how to explain this delicately. "We'd been seen together and…."

"Cat's away, the mice do play," Peter grumbled.

"You're a fine one to talk!"

"So the fellow's dead and they suspect you?"

"And some thieves stole four valuable *tikis*, and he had one of them, and now I've got it, and one of them tried to kidnap me."

"The thief or the *tiki*?"

"The thief, or maybe the murderer. I don't really know. There's been a lot going on."

"I'd better come immediately, or you may not be able to meet my plane."

"There is that possibility. But the *kahuna* and I—"

"*Kahuna*?"

"Native Hawaiian priest."

He sighed. "Not again. I thought our Spanish adventure was enough!"

"Stick with me, kid, and life will never be dull."

"So I have learned. Have you gone to the police?"

"I told you, the police suspect me of murder."

"But surely—"

"Look, I've got to run. Dinner plans."

"With whom, may I ask?"

"A charming art dealer."

"Oh," Peter replied, sounding a bit subdued.

I took pity on him. "An art dealer who is probably a crook and might be a murderer."

"Oh." He added softly, "Take care, my dear. Remember—we still have that pilgrimage road across Spain to walk!"

"Cheerio."

"Till Tuesday p.m. By the way, Noa, if something comes up and you can't meet me, leave a message at your hotel. That way I'll have a clue and can come to your rescue, riding a white charger, brandishing a sword, just like St. James the Greater."

Giggling at the thought of Peter imitating Santiago Matamoros, the patron saint of Spain, I hung up and ran down the corridor to the lobby.

Bill was waiting impatiently, tapping his expensively unobtrusive brown loafers on the marble floor, staring at the trained parrots being put through their routine for a gawking group of youngsters. When he saw me, he immediately stood up.

"Sorry for the delay," I apologized. "I just got back from Haleakala."

"Haleakala?" He repeated. "Find anything?"

I flushed. "What could I possibly find, except a breathtaking view?"

"You seem a bit flustered, my dear. And a bit worse for wear."

Just a bit. Ignoring the latter observation, I said, "I like to be on time and, unfortunately, I've kept you waiting twice now."

"Three times, if you count this morning. And it has been a very long wait."

Smiling brightly, I countered, "I'm sure you were able to keep yourself entertained. Perhaps by looking up old friends?"

He eyed me thoughtfully.

"Where shall we go for dinner?" I asked, changing the subject.

"There's a wonderful French Restaurant, Chez Paul, near Lahaina. I'd enjoy taking you there."

I shivered involuntarily. I suddenly realized I didn't want to get into a car with Bill. I didn't want to go anywhere with someone whose motives I didn't know—or rather, whose motives I did know. I wondered whether he was connected with Joe and Sam. They surely weren't intelligent enough to be working for themselves.

"Actually," I replied, trying unsuccessfully to bat my eyelashes, "I've had an exhausting day. I really would rather stay here. How about Trifles?"

"Trifles it is. Just let me cancel the reservation." He walked over to a nearby telephone, and, back turned to me, made a long phone call. Too long for simply canceling a reservation.

You had to admire the man—he was so good at pretense, he even pretended to look pleased at what was obviously an unexpected change in his plans. Whatever those plans might have been.

Dinner at Trifles was memorable, I suppose, but I was too tired to appreciate it. I do remember choosing something fishy from the English, not Japanese, side of the menu—at least I could read the words, even though I wasn't sure of the contents. And I remember telling Bill that if I wanted to fence, I'd take fencing lessons. From then on, the conversation dwindled rapidly. The dining pleasures of the evening before were a faint memory. Neither of us was up to pretending to be charming.

I was nodding off at the table when the waiter suddenly bumped into the back of my chair with the dessert cart. Instantly, I was fully awake. The collision sent a few meringues sliding off their fillings, but nothing spilled. Nonetheless, Bill berated the waiter for his carelessness and insisted the maître d' be called over. The scene that followed was most unpleasant and most indiscreet. It just goes to show that even carefully controlled masterminds like Bill have their flash points.

Two wearying hours after I had left my room, I was back. Exhausted, I propped a chair under the door handle and collapsed on the bed. In just a few minutes, I was lulled to sleep by the pounding of the surf and the gentle island breeze.

Eleven

It was a gorgeous Monday morning in paradise. No storm clouds loomed on the horizon, at least, not that I could see. Stretching languorously, I breathed in the flower-scented tropical air and listened to the distant pounding of the surf and the nearby murmur of voices.

Curious, I wrapped myself in my *pareau* and padded over to the *lanai*. My neighbors one floor below were having breakfast on the balcony. The coffee smelled delicious, but I was in no hurry to start the day.

The jangling ring of the phone shattered my mellow mood.

With a sense of dread, I picked it up. "Hello?"

"It's me, David. I must see you."

"What about?"

"The *tikis*. We must find them."

For a moment, I'd forgotten about the *tikis*. Silly me. "When do you want to meet?"

"As soon as possible. It is already 7:30 a.m.," he said, with the irritating righteousness of the habitual early riser or insomniac. Fortunately, I suffer from neither affliction.

"I need to get dressed and have breakfast. How about 9:00?" I countered, determined to salvage a little time for myself amidst the tatters of my vacation.

"Noa, this cannot wait. I will come to your room in an hour."

"Okay," I sighed, "See you then." I glanced at the notepad by the phone. Suddenly I remembered. "By the way, Robert Wiley asked me to tell you he wants to see you."

"Dr. Wiley? You know Dr. Wiley?" David replied slowly. "I wonder what he wants."

"No idea."

"I will see you soon," he said and hung up.

I tried to return Robert's call from the day before, but there was no answer.

Sorting through the wicker basket of hotel toiletry supplies, I found a packet of Hawaiian ginger bath salts. A quick soak in perfumed water removed the last of the sulfur smell that had permeated my hair and skin. Scrubbed, refreshed, and fragrant, I felt in surprisingly good spirits. Then the phone rang again.

"Yes?"

"Dr. Webster? It's Nestor. Nestor Mendoza."

"Oh. Hi," I said, unenthusiastically.

"Hi. Just wanted to see how you're doing. No more kidnap attempts? No more gunfire?"

"Not that I've noticed."

"Just checking. Wanted to make sure you're still okay."

"That's nice of you," I replied neutrally.

"Seems like the least we can do. By the way, we found out something about your friend Bill Miller."

"He's not my friend."

"Sorry. Poor choice of words. Can't you cut me a little slack? I know we started off wrong, but I'm doing my best."

He had a point. "Okay. Sorry."

"What I started to say was that Miller's got some real shady Mafia connections on the West Coast."

Somehow, I wasn't surprised. "I thought he was a 'fence.'"

"You're right. And his business contacts are some pretty dangerous people."

"Do you think the 'insurance investigators' who tried to shoot us work for him?"

"Could be. He, or one of his buddies, sure looks like a prime suspect for Alex's murderer. Try to remember: did Miller say anything incriminating last night?"

"I don't think so, but I really don't remember much of the conversation. I was very tired."

"You had a tough day yesterday, what with the kidnap attempt and all," Nestor said sympathetically.

And, I thought, he doesn't even know about the *menehune*. Or was it Madame Pele who'd come to our rescue?

He continued, "Any word from the *kahuna*?"

"As a matter of fact, he just called. He's going to meet me in an hour."

"Did you find out where they're staying?"

"Not yet. You want me to have him call you?"

He paused a moment. "There's no rush. Just give me a call later. By the way, what does he want to see you about?"

"I'm not sure," I replied, disingenuously. "He just said he wanted to talk to me."

"Alone?"

"What do you mean, alone?"

"Is he bringing his granddaughter, too?"

"I don't think so. She's got to rehearse for the *luau* tonight."

"Do me a favor, will you?"

"What?"

"Don't mention me to the *kahuna*. Just find out where I can get hold of him and his granddaughter."

"Why?" I asked suspiciously.

He hesitated, then replied, "My family's Portuguese, and a lot of the Hawaiian natives don't like *haole*. You've probably figured that out by now. Besides, they don't trust the police. You've probably figured that out by now, too. So just get me the information, and I'll pass it on to Larry, okay?"

"Okay," I said, pondering the difference between the idyllic appearance and the tension-filled reality of island life.

"Keep in touch," he said, hanging up.

I put on a pair of shorts and a T-shirt and grabbed my room key.

On the way to the hotel restaurant—not Trifles but the less-formal Raffia Room—I passed by the concierge's desk and picked up a new selection of island activity brochures. Not that I was likely to have a chance to do any of them, I thought morosely. But I could fantasize about the good time Peter and I could have had.

One side of the Raffia Room was lined with white-draped tables covered with elegantly arranged trays, baskets, and bowls, heaping with food. Brunch was being served, and I succumbed completely.

Buffets always do that to me: you have to pay for it all anyway, so you might as well eat it. And eat some more of it. Besides, I justified to myself, who knew when I'd get lunch! On top of which, I told myself, I deserved some pleasure on this trip. At least I could eat well.

Colorful banners fluttered from the high ceiling of the spacious dining room, and elaborately folded napkins and bright tablecloths repeated the rainbow. I chose a table for two next to the low, flower-topped wall; a twittering red-beaked bird flew in and perched beside me. The gilded bamboo furniture, the cool marble floors, the expanse of bright blue sky visible above the low walls, and the cheerfully chattering couples reminded me that I was supposed to be having a delightful, stress-free time at a luxury tropical resort. So much for plans.

Walking over to the buffet, I passed by the dark-haired woman I had seen on the terrace two nights ago. When she saw me, she seemed surprised, then quickly looked away. I stood in line behind a large Japanese family chatting enthusiastically, presumably planning activities for the day. An older couple came up behind me and struck up a conversation. The plump, white-haired, rosy-cheeked woman said they were from Iowa. I'd never been to Iowa, I admitted. I didn't know what I was missing, she assured me, gesturing assertively with her cane. She wore dozens of gold bracelets on her wrists, and they jingled when she moved. Her tall, slim, distinguished-looking husband smiled benignly while we talked. The line moved slowly. Bill joined the end of it and gave me a friendly wave.

The first table was laden with freshly made muffins, sweet rolls, elaborate Danishes, cream puffs, Napoleons, and nut breads. Next was a steam table with warming trays filled with eggs, bacon, spicy Portuguese sausage, and hash browns. There were also made-to-order omelets and Belgian waffles. Another table offered miniature bagels, lox, cream cheese, capers, and sliced Maui onions, cereals, and an extensive selection of sliced pineapple, mango, cantaloupe, and melon, artistically displaced in a sawtooth-cut watermelon half. Frosty glass pitchers held an assortment of fruit juices and milk.

Throwing discretion and judgment to the winds, I took some of everything. Well, almost.

While I ate, I paged through the brochures. Parasailing. Snorkeling. Romantic sunset champagne cruise on a sailing yacht. Day-trip to *Lanai*, "the Pineapple Island," featuring a down-home Hawaiian "huli-huli" barbecue. A visit to Molokai, the "Friendly Island," known for its 2,000 foot high cliffs, overgrown jungle, torrential showers, and Hawaii's highest cascade, the 1,750 foot-high Kahiwa Falls. A one-day fly-and-drive to Kauai, the "Garden Island," site of South Pacific, famous for its lush rain forest, fern grottoes, spectacular white sand beaches, majestic cliffs and canyons. A *luau*. Another *luau*. The Royal Princess *luau*, the "best *luau* on the island, featuring a stunning Polynesian review complete with Samoan fire dancers, hulas, and war canoes, and an authentic *luau* buffet, including complementary Mai Tais, *imu* ceremony and *kalua* pig, two- and three-finger *poi, lomilo-mi,* and special island sweets."

I stopped chewing my bagel in mid-bite. Lomilomi. Lomilomi. The word fluttered through my mind like a butterfly, tickling the edge of a memory. Why did it sound so familiar?

Suddenly I knew.

Lomilomi was the surname of Alex's friend Al. Trying to restrain my excitement, I asked myself: was it really possible that this unknown alimentary item was a person's last name? Of course it was, I assured myself. After all, Hawaiian names usually meant something, just as the English names Miller or Shoemaker meant something.

Al Lomilomi was the name I had been unable to remember. And Al Lomilomi was the clue to finding the *tikis*. I was sure of it.

Not even bothering to finish my coffee, I ran back to my room.

David was waiting patiently by the door.

Breathlessly, I asked, "Does the name Al Lomilomi mean anything to you?"

He shook his head.

"Could it be the name of someone?"

"Of course," he replied. "It is a native Hawaiian name. Why do you ask?"

"I think it's the name of Alex's friend. The clue to finding the *tikis*."

His usually impassive face changed; a wide, white-toothed smile brightened his face. I unlocked my room and ran to the bureau, pulling out the Maui phone book. While David peered over my shoulder, I thumbed through the tiny book. Two A. Lomilomi's were listed: Albert and Alexander.

"Which one could it be?" I asked.

He shook his head. "There is no way to know."

"How about the addresses? Do they help?"

"They might if we knew something about his friend. What did Alex say about him?"

I tried to remember. "He said Al was an old friend who 'kept an eye on things' for him. He said it several times, and each time he laughed. I remember thinking that was rather odd."

"That doesn't help."

I called each phone number, but there was no answer at either of them. Albert had an answering machine, complete with Hawaiian guitar music, but the recorded message didn't offer a clue.

Frustrated, I said, "Nobody's home; they must be at work. So what do we do next?"

"We go to their homes."

"Their homes? But nobody's there."

"This is a small island. Everybody knows their neighbors. We will soon learn where they work and go find them," he explained patiently.

"I hope this time we don't get shot at, and nobody tries to kidnap me," I grumbled.

"I hope so too. They are getting desperate. Desperation may make them careless."

"Is that good?"

"Not necessarily," he replied.

"Okay," I said grimly, realizing we really had no alternative. If we told the police, we might get killed while we tried to convince them we were telling the truth. And that wouldn't help us find the *tikis*. Besides, we still didn't know where the *tikis* were, so what could we tell the police? That I thought one of two people might possibly be a friend of Alex's?

"Let's go," I said, my voice slightly husky with emotion—or more precisely, nerves, as I dumped the contents of my evening bag into my purse.

Something was missing. With shaking hands, I explored every corner of the purse. I looked inside. No *tiki*. While David watched, puzzled, I dropped down on my knees and surveyed the floor at nose level.

No *tiki*.

I was sure I had put the *tiki* in my purse the night before. I even remembered worrying about the tiny bulge it made. So where the hell was it?

Suddenly, I remembered the scene with the waiter, the maître d', and Bill. It had seemed out of character at the time. It was. Or rather, it was completely in character—Bill had set up the confusion as a screen for stealing the *tiki*. It was a safe bet, after all, that I would have it with me since my room had already been searched twice. I had even told him about the searches. Maybe I had told him something he already knew.

Berating myself, I realized I had made it easy for him—I had been tired, dazed, almost asleep. But then I stopped berating myself. After all, Bill had planned to steal the *tiki*, one way or another. That's probably why it had taken so long to cancel the dinner reservation—he had had to make other plans.

"What is the matter?" David asked.

"The *tiki's* gone," I said, getting up from the floor.

His face tightened, and his hands started to clench and unclench. "What do you mean?" he said tensely.

Voice shaking, I repeated, "It's gone. Last night I had it, today it's gone. Bill must have stolen it at dinner."

"Bill?"

I nodded. "The 'fence.'"

David stared at me intently. "Are you sure?"

Suddenly I realized what he was thinking. "Of course I'm sure! I'm on your side, remember?"

"I am sorry," he replied. "For a moment I thought perhaps you had decided to help Bill."

"How could you think that!" I exclaimed, outraged. "After all I've been through—"

"You are sure Bill has it?" he interrupted.

I nodded.

"Then we will get it back."

"Get it back?" I said, puzzled.

"Yes. The sooner the better. Call him up," he demanded.

"Call him up? I just saw him in the breakfast line."

"Even better. Then call him to make sure he has not come back."

I called the main desk, got Bill's room number, and called. No answer.

"Where is his room?" David asked.

I deciphered the phone number code. "Conveniently, at the other end of this corridor. I guess he wanted to keep me under surveillance."

David marched out the door; I followed behind. "What are you going to do?"

"I'm going to get the *tiki*."

I followed after him.

When we reached the door to Bill's room, David tried jimmying the lock without success.

"We must get in," he growled.

"Maybe the maid will let us in," I said hopefully. "I'll make up a story."

We found the maid one floor down. She and David exchanged friendly Hawaiian greetings.

"Do you know each other?" I asked, surprised.

David nodded. "Most native Hawaiians on the island are part of a big—I think you anthropologists call it 'extended'—family. She is related by marriage to my second cousin's son."

The maid smiled warmly at the *kahuna*. "I remember meeting you at that big *luau* last year, up at Hana."

"That was some party!" David replied, laughing.

Taking a deep breath, I said, "I have a favor to ask. Would it be possible to let me into a room upstairs?"

She looked very uncomfortable, "We're not supposed to do that."

"I was afraid of that," I sighed. "The problem is . . .." I paused, then continued with feigned embarrassment, "I met this guy last night at the bar, and I went to his room—room 3004—and I left something important behind."

"Why don't you ask him for it?"

"I never want to see him again!" I replied vehemently.

"Oh?" she asked, curious.

"It's a long, unpleasant story." I grimaced, trying to look disgusted. "I don't ever want to talk about what happened! But I do want the little souvenir *tiki* I left in his room. If you would just let me in—you could even watch me look."

The maid looked nervously at David, who nodded reassuringly. I watched family loyalty trump work rules. "Okay, well, if he says it's okay, it must be. But I could lose my job for this." Leaving her cart and looking nervously around, she followed us up the stairs to Bill's room.

Heart pounding, I knocked on the door, but, as we had hoped, he had not returned.

Looking both ways, the maid unlocked the door, then whispered, "Bettah look *wiki-wiki!*"

I knew I'd better look quickly. She didn't have to tell me. While David waited to provide a diversion, if needed, I dashed inside and looked around frantically. Where to start?

Fortunately, the search was over almost immediately. Bill had left an O'Rourke's Tourist Trap bag on top of the dresser. The old "purloined letter" trick, I thought, as I peered inside. There were six small *tikis* inside. Would the real *tiki* please stand up, I thought, slightly hysterically. Taking them out of the bag, I lined them up on the table. It was immediately obvious which was the real one. Putting it in my purse, I tossed the others back in the bag and replaced it on the dresser, wondering if Bill would notice that the real *tiki* was missing.

I ran out of the room and the door locked behind me. The three of us strolled nonchalantly down the corridor. Fortunately, we met no one.

After thanking the maid for her help, David turned to me and said, "I'll meet you at your car." Then he disappeared around the corner.

I had gotten so used to David's appearing and disappearing that I didn't even ask why he didn't want to be seen with me. Or why he didn't want me to be seen with him.

I went back to my room and stuffed the phone book in my purse, next to the menacing little *tiki*. Then I headed downstairs. On the way to the car I ran into the dark-haired woman I had seen on the terrace. This time, she spoke.

"Dr. Webster?" she asked timidly.

"Yes?" I replied.

"I wonder if we could talk a moment."

"I'm sorry, but I don't have time right now. How about later?"

"I'd appreciate that a lot. When would be good for you?"

I really didn't know. "I'm going to be gone most of the day."

Shyly, she said, "I don't mean to impose. I've been trying to get up the courage . . .."

I waited impatiently.

She blurted out, "I know you're very busy, but I loved your book on the pilgrimage to Santiago, and I wondered if you'd mind autographing it for me? I knew you were giving a paper at the conference, so I brought my copy with me."

Torn between meeting David and visiting with this enthusiastic fan, I compromised. "Aren't you staying at the hotel?"

She nodded.

"Write down your name and address, and I'll get in touch as soon as I can."

"Thank you so much!" she replied, tearing out a page in her notebook and scribbling something.

I took the folded note and stuffed it in my purse, then ran out the door to the parking lot. As I rounded the corner, I thought I saw Robert Wiley walking into the hotel, but I didn't have time to stop.

Twelve

I approached the car cautiously. David suddenly stepped out from behind a column, but this time I wasn't as startled. I was learning.

"It is safe," he said, reassuringly. "There is no one else here."

"Where to?" I asked.

"We start in Lahaina. Then, if we have to, we go to Wailuku."

From reading tourist brochures, I knew that Lahaina was on the West Maui coast, a part of the island I wanted to see, famed for its luxury resorts and gorgeous tropical scenery. Lahaina was an old whaling town, filled with art galleries and upscale shopping. I might be able to do some sight-seeing after all, I mused. On second thought, probably not.

As we drove through Kihei, I saw a six-foot-tall cut-out figure of a surfer Santa Claus, complete with neon jams, rubber *zoris*, large surfboard, and sunglasses, propped up against the side of one house. A bearded, red-robed overstuffed Santa in a speedboat sleigh, pulled by six red-nosed plywood dolphins, was displayed in the front yard of another. Garish red and green elves with flashing lights on their pointed caps festooned a huge hibiscus hedge. After all, it was Christmas. Christmas in paradise.

Suddenly I felt an overwhelming nostalgia for northern New Mexico at Christmas—gently glowing luminarias lining the sidewalks, adobe houses strung with chili-pepper lights, the Three Magi parading on horseback, throwing candy to crowds, the solemn Zuni Shalako ceremony. I missed the comfort and security of my childhood, the soothing expanses of austere plateaus and eroded sandstone, the pungent smell of piñon smoke, the crisp mountain air. I'd had enough palm trees and plumerias and pounding surf to last for years. And enough *tikis* to last a lifetime.

We followed the coast road past blocks of ugly high-rise condos that blocked the view of the houses on the other side. It was easy to tell which was the pricey side of the road. Kihei straggled to an end, and the road split. The right-hand fork went across the isthmus towards Kahului, the left followed the coast to Lahaina.

We continued past a bird sanctuary filled with black and white birds standing motionless on long, pink, stilt-like legs in the shallow pond water. In the distance I could see a few masts jutting through the palm trees at Ma'alea, a popular harbor for fishermen. The road split again. The right-hand fork led north to Wailuki; our route continued west along the coast.

Traffic thickened immediately. A car swung into traffic from behind a blind corner, and a dozen horns beeped in response. We were clearly back on the tourist circuit.

On the left side of the road was the gently swelling ocean; on the right were the jagged, emerald green West Maui Mountains, shrouded by low clouds. Like Haleakala, the West Maui Mountains are volcanic, but they are older and only half as high, worn down by centuries of heavy rainfall—as much as 400 inches per year in some places. Age hasn't gentled them, however. Instead, it has created nearly vertical hillsides separated by steeply eroded canyons. As we drove by, the craggy hills and deep sensuous clefts slid rhythmically in and out of view.

The road began to climb. Mesh screens were stretched across the dynamited rock face, but even so, there were frequent warning signs: "Beware of Falling Rocks." Up close, the velvet green of the mountains was marred by long, black gashes. Ah, progress.

Just before we reached a tunnel blasted through the lava, we passed a scenic pull-off overlooking the ocean below. I skipped it without regrets.

David commented, "This is a good place to see whales."

Whales. I really wanted to see whales. I wanted to take a whale-watching cruise out of Lahaina and see humpback whales spout. Maybe there would be a chance to do so, I fantasized. We'd find the right Al Lomilomi on the first try. He'd solve the mystery of the missing *tikis*, and I would be able to spend the last day before the conference as a tourist instead of a sleuth. Fat chance.

The road sloped down again to sea level, and we drove past thickets of ironwood and gnarled *kiawe*. Suddenly I saw a sign for a roadside park and pulled off. The area was obviously popular with the locals since several beat-up pickup trucks, as opposed to bright new rented convertibles, were already parked there. While David strolled along the white sand beach, I located the toilet facilities. I'm good at that; it's sort of like a sixth sense. David was waiting patiently for me when I emerged. Frowning, he motioned towards the parking area.

"I think we are being followed."

"Oh no!" I groaned. "By whom?"

"I think it is our friends from yesterday."

"Which ones?"

"The insurance agents. The ones with the guns."

"Are they coming after us?"

"No. They are waiting in their car."

If they had wanted to, I realized, they could have kidnapped me when I came out of the outhouse.

"Maybe this time they'll just follow us, not shoot us," I suggested hopefully.

The *kahuna* just shrugged.

We headed back to the car. At one edge of the parking area, shaded by overhanging ironwood trees, was a generic white rental car. I glanced inside. The driver was red headed. I repressed an urge to wave.

We jumped in our car and I pulled out into a tiny gap in the rapidly moving traffic. Tires squealing, the white rental car peeled out right behind us.

"Damn!" I muttered.

There was nothing to be done. I couldn't lose them, since there was only one road to Lahaina, and the traffic was too heavy in both directions for any fancy passing maneuvers. I began to wish I had rented a less conspicuous car.

Somewhat to my surprise, we reached the outskirts of Lahaina without any untoward incidents—no high-speed side-swiping, no attempt to force us off the road. Of course, there was a lot of traffic, so either maneuver would have been difficult, but maybe they had changed their tactics. I wondered why.

David directed me down a side street to a small, white clapboard house. Nobody was home, so we tried the neighbors. A tiny, wrinkled old Japanese lady answered our insistent knocking. When we explained we were looking for Al Lomilomi, she nodded and pointed up the road towards Lahaina.

"He's at the Justa Fluke."

"The what?"

"The Justa Fluke. A whale-watching boat."

"Where's it docked?" David asked.

"At Lahaina," she said, "but I don't remember which berth."

We thanked her and got back into the car. When we slipped back into traffic, a white rental car pushed its way in a few cars behind.

Glancing in the rearview mirror, I said, "I think they've changed their strategy. They're going to let us find the *tikis* and then they'll hit us."

"If so, we are safe for now."

"But what about later?"

"Later is later. Now is now."

David's observation was not comforting, but it was accurate.

As we approached downtown Lahaina, we passed by a 200-foot-wide banyan tree, its enormous sprawling limbs supported by a dozen trunk-like roots that had dropped from the branches. Traffic was moving so slowly that I had plenty of time to count.

"Is that the harbor?" I asked, pointing towards some small boats bobbing up and down.

"Yes. Now you must find a place to park."

We crept past a red-roofed, veranda-wrapped, two-story hotel called the Pioneer Inn. It looked slightly seedy, which probably meant that it was authentic, but it was hard to tell on Maui—it might have been some modern developer's idea of what an authentic, slightly seedy harbor hotel should look like. Perched on the shore about a block away was an old-fashioned white lighthouse. Next to it was an achingly graceful sailing ship, white pennants fluttering from its twin masts. It was too beautiful to be authentic, I thought—it must be a reproduction.

Traffic slowed to a jerky crawl as we inched down Front Street. Cars everywhere. Parking spots nonexistent. The street was lined on either side with art galleries and curio shops, T-shirt shacks and jewelry stores, fast-food eateries and "fine dining establishments." The variety was endless and yet somehow repetitive.

Just then a car pulled out of a tiny parking space in front of us. I slammed on the brakes and pulled into the vacated spot.

The only good thing about the congestion was that the car tailing us had nowhere to park. But I knew that my relief would be short-lived. In a moment, presumably, Sam would hop out.

We ran across the street, hoping to lose Sam in the crowd. I enjoy shopping, especially in unusual places, and it would have been fun to explore some of the stores at length, but this was not the time. I glanced longingly at window displays of museum-quality jade carvings, bronze whale statues, strands of fresh-water pearls, interspersed with gaudy "Happiness is getting Lei'd in Hawaii" T-shirts. We slipped down an alley and headed back towards the harbor.

A gaily painted sign announced "Sunset Cruises, Berth #4."

A blond, blue-eyed, tanned, beautifully muscled ticket-taker lounged in a deck chair behind the sign.

I asked, "Know where we can find the 'Justa Fluke'?"

He nodded. "Half-way down, berth #22. But better hurry. She's due to sail any minute!"

"Thanks," I said, as we took off running down the sidewalk.

Berth #22 proclaimed "Whale Society Adventures: Guaranteed whale sighting with experienced naturalists." A line of barefoot passengers, shoes in hand, stood waiting patiently to get on board a large sailing yacht.

Pushing my way through the line to the ticket stand, I asked, "Is Al Lomilomi here?"

The blond, blue-eyed, tanned, beautifully muscled ticket-taker—why do they all look alike? I wondered—replied, "He's on board."

"I've got to talk with him!" I exclaimed.

"Lady," he explained patiently, "You'll simply have to wait till we get back. You can see we're about to sail."

"But I can't wait—"

He shook his head. "I'm sorry, but there's no way you can talk to Al—unless you want to come along for the ride."

I weighed our options. If we went on the excursion, we'd be safe from Sam and Joe. Even if they came along—they couldn't kidnap us. They wouldn't shoot us, and there would be too many witnesses for them to risk pushing us overboard. Besides, we'd get to talk to Al Lomilomi. And, last but not least, I'd get to see whales.

With a grin, I replied, "No problem. How much?"

"One?

I gestured towards David, waiting politely at the end of the line. "Two."

"$60.00."

"Do you take Visa?"

"Of course."

Soon we also were waiting, shoes in hands, to get on board. Sam and Joe conferred in the shade of the trees nearby and apparently decided not to join the excursion. After all, they didn't have to—they would know exactly where to find us when we returned. With a happy sigh, I decided to worry about them later.

We dropped our shoes in a large plastic tub by the gangplank and then found a place to sit half-way between the bow and the stern. Our fellow whale watchers were a typical assortment of Hawaiian tourists, most of the kids proudly sporting Maui T-shirts with mildly suggestive double entendres blazoned across the front and neon surfer shorts; most of the adults looking slightly sunburned and seriously determined to enjoy themselves.

The ship was just about to sail when a shout from the shore stopped everything. Soon the white-haired couple from Iowa struggled up the hastily replaced gangplank. For an elderly couple, they sure got around. The woman waved her cane at me, smiled, and then she and her husband sat down directly across from David and me.

On one side of us was a young couple wearing matching "Just Mauied" T-shirts; on the other side was a family with three little kids. The kids stared at David unabashed; he was probably one of the few elderly Hawaiians they had seen up close.

The four-man, one-woman crew was all blond, tan, and blue eyed, except for one fellow with curly dark hair and dark-brown skin. That must be Al, I figured. They introduced themselves and confirmed my guess. Then they took up stations on either end of the yacht and down below in the hold. Al went below. But that was all right, we'd have plenty of opportunities later on.

Bill, the ticket-taker, came on board last. He gave us a short lecture on boat safety: hold on to the railing when moving around; bare feet are less dangerous than shoes; if you feel sick, let the crew know immediately—they had a secret cure. Then Jim, the leader, treated us to an introductory discourse on the Whale Society. By chance, or should I say fluke?—we were on a whale-watching excursion run by a society devoted to preserving the whales.

Although we were on a 50-foot sailing yacht, Jim explained, they would be using the motor. It was more reliable, even if it was less picturesque. To the slosh of water and the cough-cough-chug of the motor, we set out in the general direction of the island of *Lanai*. Our crew radioed other crews, and the word spread rapidly that a pod of whales had been sighted. Every boat in the vicinity was converging on the same locale. Poor whales.

Sunlight danced on the blue-green water, and cottonball clouds drifted across the pale blue sky. The boat rocked gently in the swells as the port of Lahaina faded to a white blur at the base of dark mountains.

Suddenly Jim pointed towards 10 o'clock on the horizon, and yelled, "Thar she blows!"

They really do say that, and they really do blow.

Excited, I and everyone else turned to where he pointed and saw a fountain of white spuming up against the blue sky. The ship turned towards the spout.

As we headed towards the distant spot, Jim explained, "Whales can stay submerged for up to 30 minutes. When they surface, they exhale or 'blow' to clear the water from their twin nostrils. That's the spout you see."

We all oohed and ahhed at these fascinating facts.

Pleased, he continued. "About 500 North Pacific humpbacks migrate thousands of miles from coastal Alaska to Hawaii every winter. They come here to give birth to their babies. Each calf weights approximately 2000 pounds at birth, and the mother carries that baby for up to 11 months. Just think of that, ladies! Although we have studied the whales intensively, nobody has ever seen a mother give birth."

I found it oddly comforting that the whales were able to maintain some privacy in their lives, even with all of us watching.

"The humpback is named for their large dorsal fin, which sticks up when it dives. It has two huge 15-foot flippers, which are its pectoral fins, and a tail or fluke that can measure up to 18 feet from tip to tip. Each whale has distinctive white markings, so we can recognize individuals.

"The adults average 45 feet long and a svelte 40 tons. Humpbacks are baleen whales. They strain their food, mainly shrimp-like krill, through sheets of baleen hanging down in their mouths. But during the six months they are in Hawaiian waters, they generally don't eat. Instead, they live off their blubber. How about that for a diet regime!"

The captive audience laughed appreciatively.

"Any questions?"

"Yes!" said the lady from Iowa. "What's your secret cure for sea sickness?"

Jim pretended he didn't want to tell, but then pointed to the gray knit bands on his wrists. "See this? It's an ancient acupuncture treatment. There's a little round knob on each band, and it presses into a pressure point on the inside of each wrist. Guaranteed effective, but only if you put them on before you get sick."

Someone else asked, "And if you're already feeling sick?"

"We recommend an ice-cold can of pop or beer pressed to the neck, just below the ear. Helps deaden the nerves." He looked around anxiously. "Anybody feeling sick?"

Voices from all sides replied firmly, "No!"

He pretended to wipe sweat from his forehead. "That's a relief. If you do, make sure you're facing downwind!"

With the crew's help, we sighted more spouts, and soon tourists joined crew members in shouting excitedly, "Thar she blows at 10 o'clock!" "At 12 o'clock!"

We were approaching a pod of at least six whales. At last we got close enough— a mere 100 yards away or so— to see a whale up fairly close. The Iowa couple lent me their binoculars so I could get a clearer view.

The humpback whale looked like a fat cigar, plump in the middle and tapered at both ends. Its long slit of a mouth, which ended in a slight upturned curl, was located about 1/4 of the way down from the top of its broad, knob-encrusted head. A huge, pouch-like throat hung down below. The whale's underside was corrugated, with deep furrows extending from its throat to its belly. Mottled dark bluish-gray and white, with a ridged belly and a permanent goofy grin, the great mammal looked nothing at all like Moby Dick.

Let me tell you, it was big. Even from far away, it was big. Big and incredibly powerful—the enormous beast leaped out of the water as effortlessly as a flying fish, twisted gracefully in mid-air, and plunged back down, landing on its back. A thunderous splash reverberated through the air.

The little kid next to me was watching open-mouthed. He jumped back in fright at the explosive sound, then laughed nervously.

"In case you're wondering," Jim explained, "We don't know why the whales breach. Maybe it's to communicate to other whales. Maybe it's a way to get rid of itchy barnacles. Or maybe, just maybe, the whale is just having fun!"

Another humpback surfaced nearby, and the two huge mammals started to play. At least that's what it seemed like to me. One would arch its enormous tail, then slap the water with its flukes, making a loud splash. The other would do the same. The first one repeated this tail display once, twice, three times—a total of 18 times—while we counted aloud in unison. A record, the crew assured us.

After a while, the whales seemed to tire of their game, or maybe of their audience, and they disappeared. We waited five, ten minutes. Were they holding their breath beneath us? The restless whale watchers began to mutter impatiently.

In response, Jim said, "We have turned on some very powerful hydrophones. If we're all very quiet, we may be able to hear the whales singing underwater. Each year, the songs change and the whales learn a new one."

I hadn't expected the whales to be so trendy.

We listened intently. After a few minutes, we heard some very strange moans, grunts, chirps, whistles, and clicks, in what appeared to be random order.

The radio crackled and hissed, and then a garbled message was received. After a brief conversation with the other crew members, Jim announced that we were heading off to another sighting. As the boat turned towards *Lanai*, Al took up a post on our side of the ship.

We approached him immediately.

"Excuse me," I started, but David surprised me by interrupting. He immediately began talking pidgin. Since I couldn't understand the jargon very well, I concentrated on watching their expressions. The *kahuna* looked solemn and somehow officious; Al looked in turn friendly, puzzled, surprised, and apologetic.

With a shrug, he said, "Sorry, Brah, not me."

David turned to me. "He says he's never heard of Alex Bainbridge. Or Alexander James Cook. And I believe him."

"Why?" I asked, not out of suspicion but out of curiosity.

"He knows I am a *kahuna*, and he is a follower of the old ways. He would not lie."

He wouldn't, I thought, but would the *kahuna*? So much to take on faith, I thought, wearily, then looked out to sea.

"Thar she blows at 3 o'clock!" I shouted, and temporarily forgot my misgivings while I watched the incredible gymnastics of these gentle giants frolicking in the vast ocean.

It was both awesome and deeply moving. Intelligent, enormous, peaceful creatures, nearly hunted to extinction, barely surviving against the rapacious, thoughtless cruelty of humans. Their natural life span was about the same as ours, yet how many would get to live that long? Family groups, little babies swimming alongside their mothers, making up songs, playing games . . ..

With a shiver, I stared at the giant beasts, hoping that they, and I, would survive for another year.

All too soon, the two-hour whale-sighting excursion was over, and the Justa Fluke headed back to shore.

Thirteen

As we approached the dock, the crew offered a profusion of "Wanda the Humpback Whale" and "Have a Whale of a Time in Maui" T-shirts for sale. I declined to buy. It seemed tacky, somehow, to have the powerful, impressive beast cavorting across my chest.

We filed off the boat and for a moment it seemed as if the earth were rocking under my feet. It was no earthquake, however; my body had adjusted to the gently rolling sea and expected the land to do the same. Was this what "sea legs" meant?

While we waited our turn to hunt in the plastic tub for our shoes, Sam and Joe got up from a shaded bench under the banyan tree and strolled towards us. Then they stopped. Apparently they intended to get close but not too close.

Turned to David, I asked, "Any suggestions?"

"We ignore them. We go find the Al Lomilomi who lives in Wailuku."

I groaned. "Now? Without stopping for lunch?"

"We must not waste time."

"Eating is not a waste of time, it's a necessity!" I complained.

"I know a place in Wailuku."

"Okay," I grumbled, torn between rapidly dropping blood sugar and curiosity about where the locals eat, "But I need to eat something now."

On the way back to the car, we passed a Lappert's Gourmet Ice Cream store, and I ducked inside; David followed.

While we waited in line, Sam and Joe waited across the street. Gleefully, I thought—if we aren't stopping for lunch, neither are they. But then I realized they'd probably eaten already. A real meal. Salivating at the thought, I ordered a double-dip macadamia-nut Kona-coffee chocolate-bit ice cream in a crunchy waffle cone. David declined my offer to treat him.

Careful not to drip ice cream on the upholstery—in Maui, ice cream melts fast—I slid into the car and we started back down the coast road to the Wailuku turnoff. Wailuku was on the other side of the West Maui Mountains, and it would have been logical to simply continue around the island, past Lahaina, past the luxury resort areas of Ka'anapali and Napili, finally arriving at historic Wailuku—a scenic locale once bathed in the blood of warriors slain in battle with King Kamehameha the Great, now the tranquil Maui county seat.

But the road didn't go around the West Maui Mountains. Or rather, it did. Sort of. But whether it did or not was irrelevant: the car rental agreement I had signed specifically excluded insurance coverage if I took the car on the unpaved, coastal road. Just like the Haleakala side of the island, traffic was shunted back on itself. Good for the privacy of the locals, bad for the convenience of tourists. At least somebody still has the right priorities.

We headed back down the coast road. For a while, I thought we had lost Sam and Joe, but no such luck. They caught up with us as we drove north across the flat isthmus on Rte. 30. On the east, across the narrow isthmus, was Haleakala, its 10,000-foot summit peeking up above the clouds. On the west were acres and acres of grid-like pineapple fields, the plantings extending into the lower elevations of the West Maui Mountains.

They say that if you don't like the weather in one part of Maui, all you have to do is drive for fifteen minutes and find weather more to your liking. They say correctly. The day went from dazzling sunshine to dreary overcast in a matter of miles. And then it started to drizzle. When the rain stopped a few minutes later, a double rainbow arched between the verdant peaks. The air smelled faintly of salt water and damp earth, with just a hint of plumeria blossoms.

"Isn't it gorgeous!" I exclaimed, temporarily forgetting the danger of our situation.

David smiled. "That is why Maui is called the Rainbow Island."

How changeable it was—and diverse. Beaches, cattle, cactus, pine forests, lava flows, emerald-carpeted hills. Sapphire-blue sky, burnt-gold sun, bottle-green sea. Hot sun, warm rain. And double rainbows. Although I still wished I were in austere New Mexico, I was beginning to appreciate the island's effusive beauty.

Soon we drove by a number of scenic bungalows, gardens brimming with tropical foliage, and then past the old Kaahumana church, with its New England clock-tower steeple. We had reached downtown Wailuku, a hilly hodgepodge of high-rise county office buildings and low-rise shops. Eelskin purse outlets. T-shirt factories. Antiques. Gold sold by the ounce and the inch. The Trader of the Lost Arts imports. Thai restaurants. Fish markets. Bakeries.

"Where to?"

David was watching the street signs. "Turn here."

We headed down a one-way street, past health food stores and New Age outlets, to an old two-story house. Sam and Joe waited a half-block away. I decided to take David's advice and not worry about them. Besides, worrying about them wouldn't make any difference. Exploring one's options only works when you have them.

We knocked, and an elderly Asian lady came to the door. She was dressed in a long muumuu trimmed with lace and still carrying her quilting project, a yellow-and-white starburst pillow cover.

Her smile was open and curious.

"Hello," I said, with what I hoped was an equally engaging smile, "We're looking for Al Lomilomi."

"He's at work," she replied.

"Where's that?" I asked.

"He's a park ranger at Iao's Needle."

"Thanks very much," I said, trying not to sound disappointed, and turned away.

"Want to leave a message?" she asked, barely restraining her curiosity.

"No thanks," I said as I got back into the car.

I turned to David. "Where's Iao's Needle?"

"Back the direction we came from."

Just as I started the car, the woman came running out to the street. "If you need to get hold of Al right away, he's probably still at lunch."

"Do you know where?" I asked.

"He always eats at the same place. Harriet's."

David said, *"Mahalo!"*

"Mele Kalikimaka!" the lady replied and waved as we drove off.

David pointed in the direction of downtown. "Harriet's is the best restaurant in Wailuku. It is where I planned to take you for lunch."

Harriet's was located on a narrow one-way street overlooking a parking lot. From the outside, Harriet's was not a very inviting establishment. The big plate glass windows were streaked, and the faded banner proclaiming *"Mele Kalikimaka* and *Hauoli Makahiki Hau"* looked as if it had been used a few too many New Years.

We pushed open the creaking door and stepped inside. Two cavernous rooms were filled with vinyl-topped tables and old-fashioned red vinyl chairs. Brown vinyl booths lined one wall. Suspended from the ceiling was a large blackboard, announcing the specials of the day, most of which had been scratched out.

When we walked into the large dining room, the gum-chewing waitress greeted David warmly.

"Aloha!" she said. "Long time no see!"

He smiled. "You still got oxtail soup?"

"You betcha!"

"Oxtail soup?" I asked skeptically.

"Oxtail soup," the slightly frowsy blond waitress assured me. According to her pink and gold nametag, her name was Alice. She steered us to a table by the window.

"We are in luck, " David said to me. "Usually you have to wait in line."

I looked for someone in a Park Service uniform. Or any uniform. After all, I didn't know what a Hawaiian park ranger uniform looked like.

"You know Al Lomilomi?" David asked the waitress.

Pointing towards a slim, dark-haired man in a green uniform, she said, "That's him."

"Mahalo," David said and walked towards him. I followed behind.

"Al Lomilomi?" David asked.

"That's me. What can I do for you?" Al asked.

"You a friend of Alexander Bainbridge?"

He shook his head.

"How about Alexander James Cook?" I interjected.

He shook his head again. "First name's familiar, though."

"He was murdered Saturday," I interjected.

Startled, he replied, "That's right! I read about it in the papers. Dude got his head bashed in at some fancy hotel. But why ask me?"

David explained, "He said he was going to visit an old friend, Al Lomilomi."

"That's me all right, but I don't know him. Never met him." He shifted uncomfortably on the seat. "Must be another Al Lomilomi."

"There are only two of you listed in the phone book," I said," And we've already talked to the other one."

Alice had been waiting patiently, but now she interrupted, "You want to order or what?"

Al gestured towards the opposite side of the booth. "Why don't you join me?"

We slid in. On David's advice, I ordered oxtail soup. After all, I'd trusted him this far.

While we waited for our food to arrive, we quizzed Al about the mysterious and apparently non-existent Al Lomilomi who was a friend of Alex's.

Al said, "There are only two Al Lomilomi's on the island. I ought to know. I've lived here all my life. So have my ancestors."

Alice brought our food and Al's bill.

He wiped his mouth with the napkin and stood up. "Sorry I couldn't help. Been nice visiting, but I gotta get back to the Needle!"

"Thanks for your help," I said. *"Mahalo."*

He smiled and wiggled his fist at us, thumb and little finger extended, middle fingers folded down into the palm. "Mo'bettah you forget this Al and have good time on island! Aloha!"

"Aloha," we replied.

I asked David about the hand gesture, which I'd seen on several T-shirts, a number of signs, and lots of brochures. He explained it was called *"shaka"* and meant "Awesome, "Hang loose," "Don't worry," "Be cool." "Hang loose"? What a pleasant concept. Maybe someday—but clearly, now was not the time.

Our oxtail soup arrived, fragrant with herbs, laden with huge chunks of meat and vegetables, with a bowl of rice and spicy pickled vegetables served on the side. The interview with Al had been disappointing, but Harriet's food was not.

"What next?" I asked David, between slurps.

He shrugged. "I do not know. Are you sure you have remembered the correct name?"

"We found two of them, didn't we?" I replied defensively. "The name's correct. We just haven't found the right one."

"Maybe Melemele will remember something."

"Isn't she dancing at tonight's *luau*?"

He nodded. "Yes, but we can talk with her after the *luau*."

"I'd really like to go to a *luau*," I said wistfully.

"Good. Then we can talk to her during the break. I will meet you there."

"Sounds good to me!" I looked at my watch. It was 2:00 p.m. "When does it start?"

"At 5:00."

"Okay. It's a deal. But what should we do in the meantime?"

Shaking his head, David said, "I do not know. You are the only one who knows how to find the *tikis*."

"And I don't seem to know what it is I'm supposed to know. Maybe Melemele can help," I said doubtfully, remembering our previous lack of success in getting her to remember anything. With a start, I remembered what Nestor had asked me to do. "By the way, the police want to know where you and Melemele are staying."

"The police?" David said with a worried frown.

"They want to talk to you about the kidnap attempt and the shooting on the lava flow. By the way, how's your arm?"

Impatiently, he replied, "Fine. But who told them? You promised me—"

"The fisherman told them; I didn't. Anyway, where are you staying?"

"With friends."

"With friends? Where?"

David looked away from me for a moment, then replied, "I don't want anyone to know. It is too dangerous."

"Look," I said angrily, "I'm risking my life to find the *tikis* but you don't trust me with your address?"

"You are right. But you must tell no one except the police. It is too dangerous."

"Why is it too dangerous?"

"You ask that?" he replied, eyes widened. "You have seen what these people will do to get the *tikis*. They will kidnap, they will murder—"

"Don't remind me," I said. "I get the idea. I promise to tell no one but the police. Where are you staying?"

"Kamehameha Road."

"That's it? Kamehameha Road?"

"In the house of the Tonga family. The police will know."

"Is there a phone?"

He looked at me in surprise. "Of course not."

"Well, how about a cell phone?"

He shook his head. "Coverage is very poor. Besides, why should we want to always be available? It interferes too much."

"With what?"

"With living. Besides, people talk a lot and say nothing. You think about it."

He was right, of course. Why else had I left my cell phone behind when I came to Maui? I wanted to be on vacation. To get away from the demanding intrusion of a ringing cell phone. I wanted to be in "the here and now." It had seemed like a good idea at the time, but at the time I hadn't expected to be oscillating between hunter and hunted. There were times in the last day or two when a cell phone would have been helpful. Or maybe not. After all, the police had warned me that coverage was spotty.

Alice brought a tray of fresh fruit pies, and I couldn't resist the macadamia-nut cream pie with the coconut-sprinkled meringue topping. After all, I rationalized, life is too short to worry about a few calories. And I had a bad feeling that life might be even shorter than I thought.

Fourteen

Back at the hotel, I sneaked up the garden trail to my room. Unfortunately, so did Sam and Joe.

They came at me from both ends of the corridor while I was unlocking my door. I thought about screaming, but that seemed ridiculous. After all, they weren't threatening me. Yet. And unless you're a little kid with an attitude, it's hard to scream without an immediate incentive.

"Okay, guys, what do you want this time?" I asked, trying to sound bored.

Joe said, "We wanna work out a deal."

They kept coming towards me. "Stop right there!" I demanded, "Or I'll scream."

"Now, don't do that. We don't wanna cause no trouble," Joe pleaded.

"Oh yeah?" I snarled, in my best Lauren Bacall imitation. They didn't look convinced.

"Yeah," Sam replied, holding his arm a bit stiffly. "We got similar interests, so why don't we work together?"

"Yeah," Joe repeated.

Glancing both ways, Sam started to reach under his jacket. Was he going for his gun?

Just then, a large, noisy family came down the corridor, the little kids running on ahead. As they darted past us, I slipped into my room, leaving the two goons on the other side of the locked door. Heart pounding, I propped a chair under the doorknob. They knocked a few times, then quit.

After a few minutes of deep, measured breathing, I felt calmer. Calm enough to notice something was different in my room. This time it was something pleasant: an enormous arrangement of exotic protea on the table.

I opened the gold-edged envelope elegantly perched in the middle of the bouquet. The note read, "Thinking of you, Bill." Was there an asp hidden in the midst of the huge blossoms, I wondered?

Protea are very strange plants. When they're fresh, they look dried; when they're dried, they look fake. Named after the Greek god Protea, who assumed many guises, protea come in more than 1400 varieties, all different. The protea in the bouquet resembled fluffy pink feather dusters, large yellow plastic-bristled bottle brushes, golf-ball-size orange pincushions adorned with stiff zigzag leaves, and surrealistic peach-colored artichoke hearts surrounded by delicate petals. A few stalks of blood-red Hawaiian torch ginger completed the arrangement. There was no asp.

In a land where orchids literally grow on trees, one has to look hard to find an eye-catching gift. Mr. Miller had succeeded. I couldn't fault his taste, even if I did question his motives.

The light was blinking on my phone. Another urgent call from Nestor. A message from Bill, asking me to call as soon as I got back.

He'd know when that was, I thought cynically, assuming Sam and Joe had told him. Another from Robert, asking me to get in touch with him as soon as possible. A message from Dennis, the organizer of the conference session I was in, and another one from Chris, one of my colleagues, suggesting we get together after dinner tonight. With a shock, I realized the conference started in just a few days. The troops were gathering. And where was I? Hiding in the trenches? Lost behind enemy lines?

I called Nestor and told him where David and Melemele were staying. He thanked me warmly and assured me there was nothing new to report on the murder inquiry. Then I called Dennis, who was out, and Chris, who was also out. Probably out together, enjoying the friendly *Aloha* spirit of the island. If they only knew.

Next I called the concierge and made arrangements for a ticket to the *luau* at the Royal Princess. I was in luck: there were a few tickets left. How much? I gasped, then sighed. Oh well, I was on vacation in Paradise, right? Funny how expensive it was to live in paradise. It would have been more fun to go to the *luau* with someone, but at least I was going to go.

I called Robert, who was out, but the person with whom he was staying said Robert wanted to tell me something I needed to know about the *kahuna*. What, I wondered nervously. Last, but definitely not least, I called Bill.

"Thanks for calling me back so promptly," he said. "Did you get my little gift?"

"The flowers are lovely, but what's the occasion?" I replied, guardedly.

"No occasion. Just a gesture of good will."

"So why did you have your goons follow us all day?" I snarled, trying to catch him off guard.

"Goons?" he asked, managing to sound puzzled.

"Sam and Joe. You really must think I'm stupid if you thought I wouldn't make the connection!"

After a moment's silence, he said, "Noa, I would never think you're stupid. Foolish, maybe, but not stupid. But, my dear, we are wasting precious time. I am going to get the *tikis* sooner or later, so why not sooner? And less traumatically?"

"What makes you think you'll get the *tikis*?"

"Ah, my dear, till I met you I never knew what I was missing."

"What you're missing?" I probed, wondering if he really knew what he was missing.

"Yes indeed. Of course, it is one thing to get the *tikis*, another to keep them, as you have undoubtedly discovered."

"Right," I agreed cautiously.

"Suffice it to say I would much prefer to have you on my side. For your sake as well as mine. So I suggest we join forces."

"What exactly do you have in mind?" I said.

"You help me by finding the *tikis*, and I help you by ensuring your safety."

"And how do you do that?" I retorted. "By having your henchmen try to kidnap me? And shoot David?" I knew I sounded like a moll in a B movie, but I didn't care.

"What you have told me fills me with distress," he murmured.

"I bet," I sneered.

"Believe me, I do not approve of bloodshed. Well, let bygones be bygones. How about a deal? I'll even sweeten it with a generous monetary gesture of appreciation."

"There's nothing to deal!" I said, slamming down the phone.

I admit it. I felt rattled. I didn't like dealing with suave, debonair crooks who were threatening to have me killed. In self defense, I took a long hot bath. The Hawaiian ginger bubble bath helped soothe my nerves. So did the scalp massage I gave myself. By the time I had dried my hair and drunk a cold Maui lager beer I'd found in the mini-fridge, I felt much more relaxed. For a few minutes, I leaned on the railing of the *lanai* and watched the surf and the windsurfers roll in. Sunbathers trying to catch some late afternoon sun still sprawled on beach chairs.

It was nearly 5 p.m. Time for the *luau* at the Royal Princess. I dressed for the occasion.

Nervously, I wished I had an escort: the *kahuna*, with his martial arts, or Larry, with his police revolver. Anybody but me alone myself. With a sigh, I opened the door and peered both ways. The corridor was empty.

Rather than skulking down deserted garden trails, I took the most visible route to the main lobby of the hotel, whistling loudly as I went. After picking up my ticket from the concierge, I debated the safest route to the *luau*. There was safety in numbers, I decided, as I joined the parade heading out the front door and down the road to the Royal Princess.

Fifteen

The *luau* grounds of the Royal Princess had been transformed. Rows of white-draped tables faced a large dance platform decorated with thatch-roofed shacks and potted poinsettias piled up in the shape of a Christmas tree. In the middle of the platform a trio played Hawaiian guitar and ukulele, and sang schmaltzy Hawaiian songs. Four pretty Hawaiian women swayed in accompaniment. The color theme was red, white, and blue—blue-and-white print shirts and white pants on the men; hip-slung *pareaus*, fuzzy red leis and headbands, and brown coconut-half-shell bras held together by ribbons on the women.

Authentic it wasn't. For some reason, I had thought I was going to a real Hawaiian *luau*. I should have known better. After all, everything else on the island resembled Hollywood fantasies of tropical paradise, so why not the Royal Princess *luau*?

I stood impatiently in the long, slow-moving line, warily watching the crowd, waiting to hand my ticket to the hostess.

"*Mahalo*," she said with a smile as she stamped my hand.

Between the beach and the platform, loincloth-clad natives were busy uncovering the rock-lined *imu* pit. They had heaped worn-looking woven mats on one side, and, while I watched, they lifted out Ti-wrapped lumps from a layer of steaming grass and leaves. Opened, the packages revealed fragrant fish, sweet potatoes, and chicken. The next layer down in the pit was a large, leaf-wrapped pig, resting on a pile of glowing stones and cooked till the meat fell off the bones. The smell of smoke and steamed Kalua pig filled the air. Even though I had eaten just a few hours before, I was suddenly hungry.

I heard someone call my name and spun around. With a sigh of relief, I recognized the dark-haired fan from breakfast.

Apologetically, I said, "I'm sorry, I've been too busy to call you."

"That's okay. I understand."

She didn't, really. Or at least I hoped she didn't, really. How could she know what I'd been doing? Nonetheless, I appreciated her tact.

"Are you here alone?" I asked.

She nodded.

"So am I," I said. "Care to join me?"

"I'd love to."

We wandered over to a table and selected seats with a good view of the entertainment but far from the immense loudspeakers. Someone else called my name, and I spotted the white-haired couple from Iowa. Moving rapidly despite her cane, the elderly lady quickly claimed two seats on the other side of the table.

It felt like "old home week," even though I didn't know anybody's name. At least their faces looked familiar. I had thought I'd be attending the *luau* by myself, but Maui really was a very small island. Somehow, that was a rather comforting thought.

As if to provide additional confirmation, I saw a familiar-looking Hawaiian serving drinks at the buffet. It was the fisherman from the lava flow. At least I thought it was, though I wasn't quite sure. He looked different in uniform.

"They serve complimentary cocktails," I reminded the group at large.

"Complimentary my foot!" the lady from Iowa replied. "We paid for them! Do you realize how much this *luau* costs?"

"About $80 a person," I replied.

She looked at me in disbelief. "You mean you paid full price?"

I changed the subject. "Would you like a drink?"

"Thank you, my dear. Make mine a Mai Tai."

Her husband replied, "Make mine fruit juice."

My companion, whose name I still didn't know because I still hadn't read the note she'd given me, and I walked over to the drink table and waited in another long line. Eventually we reached the bartender. He looked even more familiar up close.

Mechanically mixing drinks, he barely looked at the patrons. I stood in front of him for a moment before he glanced up.

"Haven't we met somewhere?" I asked.

Shrugging his shoulders, he said, "Could be."

"The lava flow yesterday?"

A big smile spread across his face. "That's right! How you guys doing?"

"Okay."

"No more excitement?"

"I wouldn't say that exactly."

"Bad for tourism, that kinda stuff," he replied.

The bartender next to him gave him a dirty look, and he said, "Gotta make drinks *wiki-wiki*. Whatcha want?"

"Three Mai Tais and one fruit juice."

"Passion fruit/guava okay?"

I nodded. He handed us the drinks with a grin, and I smiled in return.

As we walked back to our table, I caught a glimpse of a familiar-looking comb-over. Joe was sitting at a table at the other end of the *luau*. I looked around for his red-headed partner but didn't see him. That worried me, since I had thought they only traveled as a matched set. Was Joe really alone, I wondered? If so, where was Sam? Out doing something nefarious? And where was the *kahuna*? He had said he'd meet me at the *luau*.

I handed the drinks to my neighbors and sat down, determined to enjoy the evening. After all, for eighty bucks, it better be quite a show.

The food was plentiful and delicious, except for the grayish-pink *poi*, which really did taste like library paste. Not that I had ever eaten library paste, but some things you just know. And I found out what *lomilomi* was: a spicy salad of salmon, tomatoes, and onions.

Bored by the banal music, I went over to the buffet table for another drink. And another slice of papaya. David was standing there unobtrusively, looking like a busboy.

"We can talk to Melemele now, before the show," David said.

"Where should I meet you?"

"By the *imu* pit."

He slipped away and I went to get my drink, then strolled nonchalantly over to the still-steaming rock-lined oven. David was waiting with an obviously nervous Melemele.

"I gotta go real soon, Grandfather, or I'll get in trouble with my boss."

Sternly, he replied, "We need your help, Melemele. We have not been able to find Alex's friend, Al Lomilomi."

"It's a matter of life and death," I added dramatically.

"I don't know anything!" she protested. "I've thought and thought, and I can't think of anything."

"Maybe it would help if we knew more about Alex," I said. "I know this must be painful, but—"

Dark, pain-filled eyes stared at me. "I don't know anything."

The *kahuna* said, "You must think!"

I tried another tactic. "Let me tell you what Alex told me, and maybe you'll remember something." I closed my eyes, trying to recreate the times Alex had mentioned his friend Al. "He told me his friend Al Lomilomi was 'looking after things' for him."

Melemele shook her beautiful head; her loose black hair rippled like silk across her caramel-brown shoulders.

"No ideas? Not even a glimmer?" I asked.

"Alex had a real weird sense of humor. Maybe he made the guy up." She looked around anxiously. "I gotta go!" She turned to me, nervously, "Don't leave without me!" And took off down the beach to join a group of dancers standing beside an outrigger canoe.

Melemele had been no help, no help at all. I wondered if she was hiding something. Maybe she knew more than she let on. Frustrated, I turned to David. "Does the word 'lomilomi' mean something other than salmon salad?"

"Lomi Lomi is the traditional Hawaiian massage. It is good for fatigue, aches and pains, injuries, things like that."

"Could the *tikis* be hidden in a massage school?"

"There are hundreds of massage schools on the island," David replied.

"I guess we've reached a dead end," I muttered.

"Looks like. Alexander Lomilomi of Wailuku said he knew all the Lomilomis living on the island, and there are only two: him and the whale watcher."

Thoughtfully, I stared out to sea. "So maybe Alex chose the name at random. In which case, we'll never find the *tikis*."

The lights on the stage changed color, and the emcee announced, "And now we're ready for the highlight of the evening. Ladies and gentlemen, the moment you've been waiting for—the Polynesian Review!"

David looked at me. "I will go call Alexander Lomilomi. Perhaps he has thought of something."

"I'll come with you."

"No, go back to your friends. You should not miss the rest of the show. I will return in a few minutes. I know where you are sitting."

"But—"

"Joe is also at the *luau*. If you leave, he will follow you."

He had a point. "Okay. See you in a few minutes."

He slipped unobtrusively away and I hurried back to my seat.

The sound of chanting and throbbing drums grew louder and louder.

Suddenly the announcer pointed out to sea and exclaimed, "Here they come, ladies and gentleman, the moment you have been waiting for—the Polynesian Review!"

Everyone stood up to watch as three outrigger canoes, bows decorated with huge *tiki* figures, approached the shore. From where I stood I could see fiercely grimacing, bare-breasted men in short, leafy breechcloths, wearing leafy collars and headbands, and gracefully swaying women in bikini tops and strung-shell skirts.

In one synchronized motion, the canoes landed on the beach and the dancers jumped out, men brandishing shiny spears, women beating small coconut-shell drums. They charged into the *luau* grounds and ran up and down between the tables, leg and wrist rattles jingling loudly, then jumped effortlessly onto the dance platform.

It was quite a performance, complete with agile, wild-eyed dancers leaping through flaming rings. Nervously, I kept glancing at my watch. Where was David?

Suddenly someone slipped up behind me and dropped a crumpled piece of paper on my lap. I turned around, but whoever it was had vanished. While everybody else watched a fire-eating Samoan, I unfolded the note. It had been hurriedly written, but I made out the scrawled message: "Got to talk to you alone. Urgent. M."

Why would Melemele send me such a strange message, I wondered. Shaking my head, I decided I'd find out at the intermission. In the meantime, I watched the flamboyant dance review and waited for David to return.

After half an hour, I realized the *kahuna* wasn't coming back. So I made up an excuse to my companions and went to call Al Lomilomi.

Patiently, he repeated the conversation he had had with him half an hour before. He had assured David that there were no other living Al Lomilomis on the island. However, there was at least one dead one: his grandfather, Alberto Lomilomi, who was buried at the Keawala'i church at Makena. I thanked him and hung up.

We had indeed reached a dead end: the graveyard.

Suddenly I knew. The *kahuna* had found out where the *tikis* were hidden and had gone to get them. Without me. Without Melemele. But why did he go without us? Was he trying to keep us out of trouble or was he double-crossing me?

I looked around the audience. Joe was still there, staring at the *hula* dancers with rapt attention.

Somehow, I had to talk to Melemele, but how? She and several other dancers were standing in the middle of the dance platform giving *hula* lessons to all the eager *wahines*. With a grimace of distaste, I climbed on stage and pushed my way through the throng to stand next to her. Then I bent my knees, stretched out my arms, and tried my best to mimic Melemele's graceful swaying.

Startled though she was by my sudden appearance, she didn't miss a beat.

I whispered, "Your grandfather's gone alone to the Makena cemetery to find the *tikis*."

She glanced at me, eyes wide with anxiety.

"I'm going after him," I said.

Her face set in a frozen stage smile, she muttered between clenched teeth, "Wait till the show is over!"

"I can't!" I hissed. "He may be in danger!" Besides, I thought, I wanted to be there when he found the *tikis*. My life might depend on it.

"Be careful," she whispered, voice thin with fear, "Don't trust anyone!"

Sixteen

Don't trust anyone? That thought had already occurred to me. Preoccupied, I stepped down from the platform and stumbled on the last step, falling into the arms of the fisherman/bartender.

"Thanks!" I gasped, after recovering my breath. "Great save."

"That's what I'm here for," he grinned.

"By the way," I said, suddenly remembering, "Why did you tell the police about the gunfire at the lava flow?"

"Me?" He replied, puzzled. "I never call police."

"You don't? I mean, you didn't?"

"Not me. I don't want *da'kine* problem. You take care, little *wahine*!" With a grin, he waggled his hand in the "hang loose" gesture.

I felt compelled to do the same, although I felt a little silly sticking out my fingers and wiggling my fist. When in Rome….

I walked over to the shaded side of the *luau* grounds to think. The *kahuna* must have taken off on foot, I realized, so I might get to the church before him if I went by car. Unless he had hitchhiked. Should I call the police? No, I decided. After all, this had to do with the missing *tikis*, not with Alex's death. On the other hand, if Joe followed us, it could get very nasty. Better cautious than dead.

Joe had his back turned towards me, so I slipped into the hotel and made a quick call. Larry was out. So was Nestor. I left a message for both of them, telling them it was urgent to meet me at the Makena church as soon as possible.

Peeking out from the phone booth, I saw no sign of Joe, so I ran back along the street to my hotel, darting behind bushes, hiding behind walls. I felt silly, but then I realized this was no time for false pride. No one waylaid me en route; no one stepped out from behind a pillar in the garage. Relieved and out of breath, I revved the car engine and took off, tires squealing.

It was still light, so I had no trouble finding my way back to the church. I drove past and parked down the road. No cars were parked on the side of the road or in the parking spot in front, and I heard no voices, so I felt confident Sam and Joe had not followed either of us.

On the far side of the church, bordered on one side by a thicket of trees, was an old cemetery, the graves outlined with lava rocks and adorned with photographs and potted flowers. Plumeria, hala, and jacaranda trees shaded the graves, effusively scenting the warm, evening air. A low lava wall separated the cemetery from the white sand beach and the sea.

I approached carefully.

The *kahuna* was standing alone in front of one of the graves.

"Find what you're looking for?" I asked snidely.

"Not yet," he replied, unperturbed.

Seething, I demanded, "Why did you run off and leave me like that!"

"I knew we were being followed," he explained, "and I hoped to find the *tikis* before the thieves found us. But since you are here, it may be too late."

"No Al Lomilomi?"

"This is his grave." He pointed to an overgrown, fern-covered plot. The faded photo marker was barely visible through the dense foliage. "But there are no *tikis*."

"You were going to steal the *tikis* yourself, weren't you?" I accused.

"How can I steal what is mine?" He replied angrily. "Anyone else violates *kapu* and deserves to die. It is the ancient Hawaiian law."

With a shiver, I said, "What about me? I've got one in my purse."

"You are different. You are trying to help." Impatiently, he looked around the graveyard. "We are wasting time. I have found the grave, but I haven't found the *tikis*."

Melemele's warning kept cycling through my mind—trust nobody. Was this what she had meant, that David would steal the *tikis*? Or did she mean something more sinister? Why was Robert Wiley, the anthropologist, also trying to warn me about the *kahuna*? I wished we'd made contact.

Torn between caution and curiosity, I approached David and the grave.

"We must find the *tikis*," he insisted. "You must help me."

"Why should I?" I replied, still angry that he had run off without me.

A gruff voice responded, "Because I'll kill you if you don't."

Brandishing his gun, Sam stepped out from behind a large fan-shaped palm. Joe pushed his way through the bushes a moment later.

Instinctively, I moved closer to David. This was probably a mistake, since it made us one target, not two.

"How did you find us?" I asked.

"Lady, we're professionals, remember. While Joe kept an eye on you at the *luau*, I staked out the hotel."

David looked as if he were preparing to spring at Sam. With a smirk, Sam said, "Don't try anything foolish, old man. I got a gun."

Taking a chance, I said, "Your boss said he doesn't like bloodshed. He told me so himself."

"Oh yeah? Well, the rules just changed."

"You find the *tikis*, we'll give you a reward," Joe said.

"A reward?" I said skeptically.

"Yeah," Sam growled, "We'll let you out of this alive. Trust me."

Remembering what had happened to Alex and what had almost happened to David, I decided not to take their word on that.

"Why should I trust you?" I challenged. "You'll kill us anyway."

"Come on, lady, we're not murderers!" Joe said.

"So you say," I replied, my voice dripping sarcasm. I wondered whether to risk flight. Would Sam shoot or wouldn't he? I decided not to find out.

Joe said, "We don't want trouble. All we want is the *tikis*."

Sam continued, "We shoulda had them to begin with, but Alex double-crossed us."

"Alex?" I gasped.

The *kahuna* muttered angrily, "Alex deserved to die!"

Startled by the venom in his voice, I turned to him. David's hands were clenched tightly, knuckles white, and his face was flushed with barely controlled rage. Instinctively, I moved way. Sam kept talking.

"Yeah, Alex. He paid us $20,000 to get the *tikis* for him, but he didn't tell us they were worth a mil! By the time we found out, he had the *tikis* and he was gone," Sam complained.

"You just can't trust nobody these days," Joe said, shaking his head.

"I guess not," I tried to sound sympathetic. "But how did Bill Miller get in on this?"

"We had to find Alex fast, before he left the islands. We'd worked with Mr. Miller before, so we called him. He's got connections, you know."

I did indeed.

My mind raced. They had brought Bill Miller into the action after the theft, unbeknownst to Alex. So Alex couldn't have been planning to meet Bill Saturday morning. Bill had lied. What else had he lied about? Was he the murderer? I didn't think so. After all, he hired goons—including these hired goons—to do the dirty work.

"Did Alex know Mr. Miller?" I asked.

"Sure. He done a lot of business with him," Joe replied.

"How did he know you?" I asked, stalling for time.

"We work for Mr. Miller. But sometimes, like this time, we done a little work on our own."

Mulling over what I had just learned, I said, "I don't suppose Mr. Miller was too happy about that, was he?"

"Huh?" Sam said.

"I bet he wasn't too happy about you 'doing a little business on the side,' so to speak. Or about Alex cutting him out of the deal."

"He was pissed all right," Joe replied.

For a moment, I was so lost in thought—remembering what Bill had said about how he hated being double-crossed—that I forgot the immediate threat of the situation. But then Sam waved his gun again and I remembered.

"Enough stalling. You better find the *tikis*! They must be here somewhere."

"Why should we help you?" I challenged. "You'll kill us anyway."

"How do you know?" Sam snarled.

"It's not 'rocket science.'" I took a risk. "You killed Alex, and now you'll kill us."

Joe replied in annoyance, "Lady, we never killed Alex. Where'd you get that idea?"

"You didn't?" I said, surprised.

"Hell no. We didn't even get here till after he was dead."

Sam added, "Besides, we wouldn't've killed him before getting the *tikis*. We're not stupid."

That was hardly reassuring. I glanced at the *kahuna*. His normally serene face was still swollen with rage and his chest was puffed out, his hands clenching and unclenching while I watched. Had he killed Alex?

"Believe me, lady," Joe said, "We just want the *tikis*. Besides, you owe us one."

"I do?" Now I was really confused.

"Who'd'ja think pulled you out of the cinder cone after the gas release?"

"It was you?"

"Who'd you think?"

I had thought it might have been Pele or the *menehune*, but I didn't feel like telling them that.

"Then why did you disappear afterwards?" I asked, puzzled.

"The boss said keep you under surveillance but stay out of sight. We always —well, almost always—do what the boss says."

"So why'd you try to kidnap me at the lava flow?"

"We thought you guys had got the *tikis*."

Sam hitched up his pants and shifted his substantial weight. "Look, lady, we ain't got all night. Quit stalling!"

He cocked his gun.

I glanced at David out of the corner of my eye. He was still staring into space, hand clenching and unclenching, muttering. Was he getting ready for a life-saving martial arts demonstration? Was he reciting a silent invocation to call down the gods? Whatever he was doing, he radiated barely controlled rage. I wasn't sure which was scarier: the *kahuna* or the gun-waving goon.

Wearily, I said, "If we knew where the *tikis* were, don't you think we would have found them by now?"

"You can't fool me," Joe said. "You ain't standing in front of that grave for nothing!"

He was right.

Under our captors' watchful eyes, David and I looked around the grave, digging through the fern fronds with our hands, shifting the lava rocks that made up the border. The cinders were small and light, but their edges were sharp. I remembered the blood we had found at the lava flow. Whose was it after all? I hadn't noticed any bandages on Joe or Sam, but maybe they hadn't cut themselves in a visible location.

Besides, what difference did it make. That attack was old history. I had something more worrisome to deal with now. Like a gun-wielding goon and an angry *kahuna* who might, or might not, have double-crossed me and murdered Alex. Hard to tell friends from foe, especially in a graveyard.

I kept as much distance between David and me as I could, and not just to make it more difficult for Sam to shoot us. There was no sound except for the rattling of the palm fronds, the grinding of lava rocks against each other, and my heavy breathing.

We found nothing except a few geckos hiding in the fronds and underneath the rocks.

Sam cocked the gun at me. Again.

Fear made me angry. "You're just a coward! First you shoot an unarmed man, and then—"

"Whatcha talking about, lady?" Sam replied.

"At the lava flow. You shot David."

He shook his head. "Not me. I never shot him."

"You didn't? Then who did?"

"Got me. We was trying to grab you, and suddenly somebody started shooting. Sam shot back." Joe pointed to his stiff shoulder. "I didn't duck in time."

But if they hadn't shot David, who had? And why?

Sam continued, "But that don't mean I won't shoot you now. Both of you, if I have to. Like I said, the rules got changed."

Joe interrupted, "Come on Sam, calm down. We got enough trouble already." He looked nervously at me. "Give us a break, okay? All we want is the *tikis*."

All we wanted was the *tikis* too. Actually, that was no longer true. We—at least I—also wanted to get out of this alive.

Would the police get my message? Would they come in time? I didn't want to bet my life on it. We were at an impasse. It was getting too dark to look much further, and besides, I was out of ideas and David wasn't offering any suggestions. Sam and Joe were huddled together, whispering ominously.

Just then I heard the faint sound of something heavy sliding onto the beach. A moment later a dozen fierce spear-waving warriors came charging over the low lava wall, filling the night with blood-curdling yells.

Seventeen

Within moments, sharpened spear points surrounded Sam and Joe. Cowering, Sam dropped his gun on the ground. One of the dancers picked it up and stuck it in his loincloth. A beautiful, *pareau*-clad dancer stepped over the lava wall and joined the group.

"We got here as fast as we could," Melemele said apologetically. "It took a while to get the gang together after the show."

Grateful, I exclaimed, "I never expected to see you here!"

"I saw Sam and Joe sneaking off, so I knew there would be trouble."

Just then the police arrived, sirens screaming, lights flashing.

Melemele turned to me, her face registering deep dismay. "Not the police! You didn't call the police!"

"Of course I did."

"But Grandfather—"

Larry Nakamura climbed out of one of the police cars, gun drawn, and looked around. Another policeman stepped out of the other side of the car. It wasn't Nestor.

"Looks like you got the situation well in hand," Larry said, nodding at the spear-wielding dancers. I felt oddly pleased.

Gesturing toward the other policeman, Larry said, "This is Ike. Ike Jones. Now, what's this all about?"

It took some time to sort out the confusion. After listening to my brief repeat of the graveside conversation—Sam and Joe had told me more than they should have, I realized—but that wouldn't have mattered, if they had planned to kill us. The police decided to take the *kahuna* in for questioning about Alex's murder, and they took Sam and Joe into custody for theft, attempted kidnap, and assault. Several more policemen had appeared by this time. After making sure nobody was armed, they handcuffed them and led them away to the waiting patrol cars. The *kahuna* went silently, impassively, eyes looking at the ground. I wanted to say something to him, but what would I say? Sorry you got caught? Don't trust anyone? Gee, you sure had me fooled?

Larry looked at me, shaking his head. "I hope this is the end of it." He continued suspiciously, "But somehow I don't think so. Tell me: what were you doing here? Grave robbing?"

With a nervous laugh, I said, "We—the *kahuna* and I—were on a wild goose chase."

"The missing *tikis*?"

I nodded. "I thought I had a clue, but it turned out I was wrong. It's a shame, but I guess the *tikis* are gone forever."

Larry said, "If you get any more bright ideas, let me know first, okay? Don't try to solve any more mysteries on your own. Relax, have a good time, enjoy Maui. 'Hang loose,' promise?"

I wiggled my hand in the *shaka* gesture. "Promise."

Larry looked at the crowd standing around. "Fun's over for the night, folks. Everybody got a way home?"

"Sure thing," the dancers replied, heading to the beached outrigger canoes.

With a friendly wave, Larry got into one of the patrol cars and sped away.

Melemele and I were left sitting alone on the crumbling lava wall in front of the grave. I listened to the distant pounding of the surf, the faint calls of the dancers, the rustling pond fronds. I breathed in the scents of paradise, mixed now with the earthy smell of the disturbed soil around Al's grave. Melemele was weeping quietly.

"You know," I said sadly, "I still can't believe your grandfather killed Alex."

"I didn't want to believe it either," she sniffled, "But who else could have done it? He and Alex had talked a lot about the *tikis*, and then they were stolen. And I told Grandfather Alex didn't want anyone to know he was here on the island. I told him we were going to elope. Grandfather must have figured that Alex took the *tikis*."

"So in a moment of rage, he killed Alex for violating *kapu*. I even heard him say at the graveyard, 'Alex deserved to die'!" I shivered, remembering the fury in his voice. "I wonder why Alex did it," I mused.

"Did what?"

"Stole the *tikis*."

Melemele thought a moment and replied, "He said he had a real special wedding gift but it wasn't for me. It was for the *kahuna*. I've been trying to figure it out. I think Alex had Sam and Joe steal the *tikis* so he could give them to Grandfather."

I listened, stunned. "A gift for the *kahuna*?"

She nodded. "Grandfather really wanted the *tikis*."

So that was it. It made perfect sense—or at least it did if you had a lot of money to spend and not a lot of scruples. Alex arranged to have the *tikis* stolen, but he hadn't realized they were so valuable. When the newspaper article came out, Alex knew he was in deep trouble. The thieves he'd hired demanded he sell the *tikis* to Bill Miller for a lot of money, or give them a lot more money for the theft, but he wouldn't do it. For one thing, he wanted to give the *tikis* to the *kahuna*, not sell them. For another thing, he didn't want to pay blackmail and—maybe—he didn't really take Sam and Joe's threat very seriously. So he decided to hide out until things cooled off. At least, that's what I was guessing.

I heard Melemele's *pareau* rustling as it rubbed against the lava wall.

"You were going to go to Hong Kong together?" I asked.

"Yes," she whispered, then cried some more.

So she was the mysterious Mrs. Bainbridge. Or she would have been.

"I'm so sorry," I said, hugging Melemele.

Melemele explained between sniffles. "I was afraid that Grandfather had killed Alex, but I couldn't tell anyone. The ancient punishment for breaking *kapu* was strangulation or head bashing. You know Grandfather believes in the old ways, and stealing the *tikis* would be real *kapu*."

I nodded, remembering the *kahuna*'s terrifying, barely controlled rage. But how had he known about the *tiki*? Had he seen Alex and me playing with it? Had Alex fled when he saw Bill Miller but run straight into the *kahuna*, who killed him before asking any questions? In which case, his story about looking for Melemele had been a fabrication. My head spinning, I realized Melemele was still talking.

"Could you repeat that? I'm sorry, my mind was wandering."

"I was afraid to warn you about Grandfather, and then I was afraid what would happen if I didn't warn you!"

No wonder she had seemed so tense and uncommunicative.

With a sigh, I patted her quivering shoulders and said reassuringly, but without conviction, "Maybe there's another explanation."

Like, maybe Bill Miller was the murderer, I thought, without really believing it.

I reached in my purse for a piece of Kleenex for Melemele and my fingers touched the *tiki* figure. Looking around the deserted graveyard, I had a sudden idea.

In a very low voice, just in case anyone was listening, I said, "Let's try to find the *tikis*."

"I thought you said it was a wild goose chase."

"I know what I said, but I just had an idea."

Slowly, I walked over behind the grave marker and faced the same way as the faded photo. Melemele came over and joined me. At the same height as the photo was the crumbling lava wall where we had been sitting. I walked back over to it and dislodged a few loosely inserted stones. Hidden behind them was a plastic shopping bag. Carefully, I pulled it free.

"Alex was right," I said softly. "Al was keeping an eye on things for him."

Wiping her tear-streaked face with the back of her hand, Melemele sniffed, "Alex always was a joker."

With great care, we opened the tape-wrapped package and pulled three six-inch-long *tiki* figures out of the dark confines of the bag. I lined them up on the lava wall. Their malignant eyes glittered red in the fading light. Rubies, I thought. Blood-red rubies.

"Now that we have found them, what are we going to do with them?"

In a small, frightened voice, Melemele said, "They've caused so much evil, I want to throw them into the sea! But I know what they mean to my grandfather and to my people. They belong with us."

"They may cause more evil yet, you know," I observed. "Bill Miller wants them very badly. It may not be safe for your people to keep them.

"But how will he know we found them?"

"Good point," I said, nodding my head. "I won't tell."

"Neither will I," she replied solemnly.

I handed the sacred *tikis* to her and she cradled the rough, dark forms gently in her arms.

Eighteen

Shifting shadows loomed over the graveyard, filling the moonlit night with a palpable sense of doom. A stiff breeze had sprung up, rattling the branches of the palm trees and shaking loose an overpowering fragrance from the nearby flowering bushes.

"Let's get out of here," I said, with a shudder.

"Will you drive me home?" Melemele asked.

"Of course. Just tell me how to get to Kamehameha Road."

"How'd you know where we're staying?"

"Your grandfather told me. I asked. Nestor wanted to know."

"Nestor? Nestor Mendoza? The policeman?" she asked in surprise.

"Yes. He wanted to talk to both of you about the incident at the lava flow." I glanced at her. "You seem surprised. Do you know Nestor?"

"I broke up with him when I started seeing Alex."

"You're the girlfriend who broke up with him?"

"Uh-huh. Nestor was awful mad at me. He scared me, he was so angry," she said with a shudder.

"What a small world," I said, shaking my head.

We walked in silence to my car and I drove back towards Kihei. Following Melemele's directions, we soon reached the shabby house where I had picked her up before. No lights were on.

"Aren't you staying with a Tonga family?"

"Yeah, but they're away visiting relatives."

"You sure you'll be okay by yourself?" I asked.

"Sure," she sniffled.

"You sure? I know you're upset about your grandfather."

Bravely, she replied, "I believe in the old traditions, but Grandfather had no right to kill somebody! Especially my fiancé," she added, breaking down again in tears.

Giving her a hug, I said, "Call me tomorrow at the hotel, okay? I'll take you to lunch or something."

"Okay. I promise."

"Good. Good night, Melemele."

"*Aloha*, Noa. *Mahalo nui loa.*"

As I drove away, I felt deeply uneasy. I glanced at the seat. Melemele had left the *tikis* behind. But that wasn't what was bothering me.

Suddenly I knew what was bothering me. The fisherman/bartender had told me he hadn't called the police. But Nestor had said he had. Or, at any rate, he hadn't contradicted me when I had said the fisherman had. So how had Nestor known about the incident at the lava flow? How, indeed, unless he had been there?

It all came together at once, like a Chinese puzzle box when all the pieces slide into place. Nestor had been at the lava flow that morning and he had fired the first shot. He'd aimed for Melemele but he'd missed and hit David instead. Sam and Joe hadn't lied—they weren't supposed to shoot anybody and they hadn't. Nestor had. And then they had shot at Nestor, and Joe had been shot in the melee. Hence the blood spots on the lava flow. Nestor's murderous jealousy had driven him to try to kill the person he had once loved.

And, working backward, I was certain that Nestor had killed Alex. He had killed Alex not because of the *tikis* but because of jealousy. I was as sure of it as if I had been there. Nestor had found Alex in the garden at the hotel, tried to talk to him about Melemele, learned they were eloping, and, in a fit of rage, killed him. I could see Alex, wealthy privileged *haole* that he was, looking in surprise at the policeman, shrugging off his questions, or answering them off-handedly, condescendingly.... Perhaps he impatiently turned away and that's when Nestor hit him with something—probably his gun—and tossed his unconscious body into the Jacuzzi.

I knew what had happened. Maybe I didn't know all the details, but I knew enough of them.

The coincidental theft of the *tikis* conveniently covered up the real motive for the murder: jealousy. The only person who could link Nestor to Alex's murder was Melemele. So Nestor had to kill her fast, before she could put two and two together and tell the police the real motive for the murder. There's nothing like a lover spurned, or like burning desire turned into consuming hate.

Tires squealing, I did a U-turn and sped back to the house where I had left Melemele. I had to warn her about the danger she was in. Nestor might come looking for her at any time. After all, I'd given him the address.

Caution took over just in time. Instead of roaring up to the front door, I parked the car a block away and, clutching a tire iron I took out of the trunk, I proceeded silently on foot. It would have been more poetic to use one of the *tikis* as a weapon, but I didn't think six inches of wooden *tiki* would make much of an impact.

Silhouetted against the darkened sky, two people stood motionless in the yard. I approached on tiptoe, my advance covered by the rattling palm fronds and the moaning of the wind.

Nestor had a large revolver pointed at Melemele. It glittered in the moonlight.

"I've tried to find you for days," he growled.

"I don't understand, Nestor," she whimpered. "Why do you want to shoot me? What have I done?"

"What have you done?" He raged. "You left me for that rich blond *haole*, that's what! I wasn't good enough for you!"

"Nestor, it wasn't like that. Really it wasn't!" She started to sob.

Snarling, he ordered, "Shut up! It's too late to come crying to me. It's your fault that I killed Alex. Now I'm going to have to kill you, too."

"You killed Alex?" she gasped.

I sneaked around behind Nestor, hiding behind palm trees. Something squished underfoot, but they didn't notice.

"Like I said, I killed Alex. I caught him running up the path at the hotel. I tried to talk to him, but he wouldn't listen. He thought he was too good to talk to me. So I bashed him in the head."

"But why do you have to kill me?" Melemele pleaded. "What did I ever do—"

"You're the link between me and Alex. I can't risk you talking. Ever. Besides, you deserve to die for what you did!" He cocked the gun and pointed it at her. "*Aloha,* Melemele."

She crumpled in a heap on the grass and began to weep. As he walked slowly towards her sobbing form, I crept up behind him, raised the tire iron, and bashed him on the back of the head. He toppled over on the ground, then started to twitch and groan. I had knocked him down but not completely out. I'd been afraid to hit him too hard, remembering how Alex had been killed.

Melemele stared at me, stunned, then jumped up and grabbed the gun from Nestor's slack fingers. She handed me the gun and ran inside the house, soon returning with a length of rope. We tied Nestor's arms behind his back and then fastened his hands to his feet, which we also tied together. He sprawled like a trussed chicken on the ground. It was an amateur job, I admit but, after all, we were amateurs.

Wiping the sweat from my forehead, I asked, "Where's the nearest phone?"

"At the Kwik Shop, a couple of blocks away."

"You sure you'll be all right if I leave you alone with him?"

"No problem. I'll kill him if he moves. And maybe, maybe, even if he doesn't."

Her mouth was twisted in a fierce grimace and her eyes were locked in a frozen glare. Long black hair blowing around her face, grass skirt whipping in the wind, bare feet planted far apart on the ground, she resembled an ancient, wrathful Hawaiian goddess.

She hissed, "He killed Alex. He deserves to die!"

"That may be," I said soothingly, "But don't do it. Try to restrain yourself."

She looked unmoved.

I tried again. "The police will need to question Nestor to clear your grandfather."

With a shiver, she blinked, then tossed the hair off her face. "You're right. For a moment I forgot. We must free Grandfather."

I left her sitting on the grass, gun aimed unwaveringly at Nestor's immobilized form.

Nineteen

The next morning I was relaxing on the *lanai*, drinking fragrant Kona coffee and scanning the sea for whales, when the phone rang. I hestitated, then, with a sigh, strolled back into the room. Maybe it was Peter, calling to tell me about a change in plans. I hoped not. He was due in later that afternoon.

"Hello?"

"Hi. This is Robert Wiley."

"Hi, Robert," I replied, pleased to hear from him at last. "I tried to call you a couple of times."

"I know. Thanks. Listen: I have to warn you about the *kahuna*."

"About the *kahuna*?" What new revelations await, I wondered.

"Right. If you see him, what ever you do, don't mention the stolen *tikis*."

"Stolen *tikis*?"

"The ones I told you about," he replied impatiently. "The ones stolen from the Culture Museum. He's got a real 'thing' about those *tikis*, and he'll blow his stack."

Laughing, I replied, "Thanks for the warning! My lips are sealed."

Just then, someone started knocking insistently on my door.

"Sorry, got to go," I said, and hung up.

What now, I wondered, as I walked over and peered through the peephole. Staring back at me were the distorted faces of Melemele and David.

"*Mele kalikimaka!*" They chorused as I opened the door.

With a smile, I said, "Merry Christmas to you, too!. I take it the case is closed and David's a free man?"

They nodded.

"The police checked on Nestor and found that he was gone at all the right—or wrong—times," Melemele explained. "And he'd filed a false report on the lava flow shooting."

"What about the *tikis*?"

"The *tikis*? What *tikis*?" David asked innocently.

"Right. What *tikis*," I replied with a smile.

David said solemnly, "I want to thank you for all you have done."

"Oh, it was nothing."

"We, my granddaughter and I, wish to hold a *luau* in your honor."

"For me? A real *luau*?" I gushed.

"Yes, a real *luau*. An authentic Hawaiian *luau*. I know you can tell the difference," he added. "We will hold it tomorrow night, if that is all right, on the beach at Makena."

"Fantastic!" Then I remembered Peter would be with me. "Do you mind if I bring a friend?"

"Of course not."

"By the way," David added, "you have something that belongs to me." He held out his hand.

I walked over to my purse and took out the *tiki*. "I wondered if you'd remember," I said, laughing.

"How could I forget? But here is something in exchange." He tossed me a small Ti-leaf-wrapped bundle.

"*Mahalo.*"

"*Mahalo nui.*"

Melemele turned back as they were leaving and waved. "*Aloha!*"

I smiled and waved back, then closed the door and walked out on the *lanai*. Then I unwrapped the package. Inside was a three-inch-long, crudely carved *tiki*, its eyes green and glowing, its white teeth sharp, its headdress resembling flames. I had never seen it before. A tourist souvenir of Madame Pele? Somehow, I knew it wasn't. As I stared at it, the menacing grimace slowly transformed into a snaggle-toothed grin.

Glossary of Hawaiian Words and Phrases

A'a: sharp, jagged, clinker-type lava that spews out partly solid and full of gasses.

Aloha: Hawaiian acknowledgment that can mean either hello or good-bye, like the Italian *caio*. Can also mean "love."

Aloha 'aina: love, respect, and stewardship of the land and waters.

Aloha kakahiaka: Good morning.

Brah: "Brother," pal.

Da'Kine: The real thing, a "Da'Kine" surfing wave, for example, or a "whatchamacallit."

Haole: Hawaiian native term for foreigner, Caucasian.

Heiau: ancient Hawaiian place of worship.

hula halau: traditional dance troop.

Hula: Hawaiian form of communication using dance. Some of the dances are considered sacred.

Imu ceremony: ceremony centering around the underground pit oven used in *luau* cooking.

Ipu: traditional Hawaiian gourd instrument.

Kahuna: Hawaiian priest, expert in a field, highly skilled person. "The Big Kahuna."

Kapu: Hawaiian for "taboo," ritually forbidden, sacred.

Kupunakane: Hawaiian for grandfather.

Lanai: balcony, porch, veranda.

Lei: traditional garland of flowers, vines, or shells. Each flower and style has a different significance.

Luau: feast featuring poi, imu-baked pork, and other traditional island food.

Mahalo: Thank you.

Mahalo nui loa: Thank you very much.

Mele Kalikimaka: Merry Christmas.

Mele Kalikimaka and Hauoli Makahiki Hau: Merry Christmas and Happy New Year.

Mele: sacred Hawaiian chant, song.

Menehune: mythical elf-like "little people" who avoid the light; legendary tiny inhabitants of the islands before the Polynesians came.

Mo'opuna: grandchild.

Pahoehoe lava: extremely hot, flowing lava that hardens like smooth pancake batter.

Panioli: cowboys, usually Spanish or Portuguese.

Pau: Done, completed, finished.

Pupu: appetizer, snack, hors d'ouevres.

Shaka: Hawaiian hand gesture with little finger and thumb wiggling, other fingers slanted down toward palm; means "awesome," "hang loose," "relax," etc.

Tapa: beaten fiber cloth, typically Polynesian.

Wahine: woman.

Wiki-wiki: Pidgin for quickly, very fast.

Elyn Aviva

Elyn Aviva earned a Ph.D. in cultural anthropology at Princeton University (1985); her dissertation topic was the modern-day pilgrimage on the Camino de Santiago in Spain. It was the first anthropological dissertation on the Camino, and *Following the Milky Way,* her travel narrative based on her experiences and her research, was the first contemporary American account of the pilgrimage. Elyn has traveled the Camino a number of times, including three times on foot (1982, 1997, and 2000). In 2002 she began walking one of the French Chemins de St. Jacques (Roads of St. James), the route that begins in Le Puy en Velay.

Elyn is a long-time student of Sufism. She has also studied geomancy and sacred geometry with a French Druid. When not traveling or living in Europe, Elyn lives in New Mexico with her husband, Gary White. They trained at Grace Cathedral in San Francisco to be labyrinth facilitators, and they lead labyrinth-walking workshops (complete with slide shows).

A pilgrim at heart, Elyn is happiest when she is doing research on and writing about sacred sites, sacred geometry, and spiritual quest. She is available for presentations on pilgrimage, the Camino de Santiago, and labyrinths. Her newest passion is creating sacred fiber art (www.fiberalchemy.com).